SO LOST
ARE
THE
FOES

NISSA HARLOW

NIMBLE HOPE PUBLISHING

ISBN: 978-1-7781397-8-9

Published in Canada by Nimble Hope Publishing
Cover and book design by Nissa Harlow

For those who help the lost find their way.

CHAPTER 1

A HOUSE AT THE END OF THE WORLD

"Maybe this isn't as bad as it looks," Viktor said. The sharp bark cut through the early morning air, making him wince and letting me know that he didn't believe his words any more than I did. Click started toward the porch steps, but Viktor reached out and laid a hand on the boy's shoulder, stopping him without another word. The three of us watched the little white dog have his tantrum up on the porch of his former home—a house that now belonged to the squiffy little pissant who'd tried to put mongrel on the dinner menu.

"And maybe it's exactly as bad as it looks," I said, keeping my voice low. Not that it was going to make much of a difference. Buddy had already given us away. I looked around for a place to hide. The huge lilac bush was probably our only option. I turned back to Viktor and fixed him with a glare that he didn't notice. His cloudy eye looked pale and dull in the dawn light as he stared at the dog on the porch. "They've got pellet guns, remember?"

"We've got pinkhands."

"They've got those, too."

He shook his head slowly, almost as if he were trying to listen. I couldn't hear much other than Buddy's whining and scratching as he made his fruitless attempts to get inside the house.

"Bah-dee," Click called, his voice soft. But the dog didn't pay him any attention.

"We can't keep bringing him with us," I muttered.

Viktor turned to me with a frown. "Who? Click?"

I gave him a look.

"Yeah. I know." He sighed and looked back up at the porch.

"This will be the third cache we've had to walk away from because he's blown our cover."

"Yeah. I know."

"I'm *hungry.*"

"You're hangry." He glanced at me with a little smile that I tried to ignore. He wasn't wrong, and my frustration level was almost at its limit.

I took in a deep breath and let it out slowly. Buddy's scratching and whining (and occasional barking) didn't seem to be getting any response. My tightly wound innards started to relax a little.

"Maybe the place is empty," Viktor said. He rose up onto his toes as if trying to get a better view.

"It's occupied." My voice was absent. I watched the pink tag on the door, waiting for a flutter that I could take as my sign to get the hell out of there. "Come on. We need to get Buddy and go. This wasn't what we came for, anyway."

"Maybe it's a sign."

"What's a sign?"

"This is one of Joshua's caches, right?"

"As far as we know."

"You don't sound so sure."

"It's kind of far from his throne room and right on the edge of his territory. Shitty place for a cache house."

"Or maybe that's what makes it a great place for a cache house." He tilted his head back to look up at the windows on the second floor. "As long as they removed the stinker."

I shuddered, remembering what we'd found in that bedroom. "If they didn't, it's going to reek in there."

"Right. So they probably did." He took a deep breath, reached up to tighten his ponytail, and strode forward. I let out a squeak.

"Viktor!"

"It's fine, Léa."

"It's not *fine*," I growled. I was already eyeing that lilac, ready to dive into its leafy branches at the first sign of trouble. "Do you want to get shot?"

In response, he made one of his raspberry noises as he lifted his right hand. A swirling vortex of pink roiled in his palm, looking out of place in the otherwise-mundane scene. I turned to Click, hoping to find that he was just as annoyed with Viktor's recklessness as I was. But as soon as I turned, he scampered after Viktor, leaving me standing on the sidewalk all by myself. My hands tightened into fists, and the crinkle of paper drew my attention to the scrap I'd forgotten I was holding. I uncrumpled it. The address, hastily scrawled in yellow highlighter, was hard to make out in the shadow from the lilac. But I knew it was *not* the address of the house in front of us. We'd taken a detour, led by a dog with a misguided sense of nostalgia.

I looked up as I realized the scratching and whining had stopped. Viktor and Click were both on the porch, and Buddy was staring up at them in anticipation.

"What are you waiting for?" I whispered as loudly as I dared. "Grab him, and let's go!"

Viktor shook his head and leaned toward the door. A second later, he had his ear pressed to it.

"Are you fucking insane?" My hiss grated in my throat. I marched to the base of the porch steps and glared up at the trio of idiots. Well, maybe Buddy got a pass; he was just a dog, after all. But Viktor and Click had lived in the Rift Zone for long enough to know better. "Let's *go!*"

Viktor shook his head as he pulled back from the door. "I don't hear anything."

"They could be in the bathroom."

"Or there might not be anyone here." He looked down at the porch and took a step back. "Nobody's been here for a while."

"What?"

"Come up here." He waved his hand toward me. I glanced around, up and down the street. If we ended up having to run, at least there wouldn't be anyone standing in our way. With a deep sigh, I began to climb the steps. "Look," Viktor said as I reached the top.

There must've been a doormat at some point. I couldn't remember if there had been one the last time we'd been there or not. But there wasn't one now. What *was* there was a slightly cleaner rectangle and a bunch of dried plant bits. A few crispy leaves were nestled against the door itself, probably blown there by the wind.

"This door hasn't been used in a while," he said.

"This is a cache house. You think they're dumb enough to use the front door when they're coming and going?"

"They're Joshua's guys."

"They're not all as stupid as he is."

"Fair point." He leaned toward the door and peered in the shallow window that ran along the top. "I don't see any movement."

I shook my head. "This isn't the cache we were supposed to hit."

"How's Ryver going to know? If we come back with something good—"

"There might not be anything in there."

"There might be something *amazing* in there."

"Face-eating dogs?"

He snorted and looked down at Buddy, who was investigating the rest of the porch.

"Viktor—"

"We're already here. We should at least check."

"We're wasting time. If we don't come back with something—"

"How do you know there's not something here?"

"How do you know there is?"

He shook his head. "The glass is half full, Léa."

"It's full of *something*," I muttered, which just made him laugh. A little too loudly. My heart surged into my throat. But I still didn't hear anything from beyond the door.

"I'll go first," he said, reaching out to grasp the doorknob. But I grabbed his arm, startling him enough to stop. "What?"

"If we disturb that"—I pointed down at the rectangular mess—"they'll know we were here."

"Right." He pulled his hand back and headed for the steps. "Back door."

"Viktor!" My urgent whisper didn't seem to have any effect. Click followed him, and Buddy—after a few more seconds of sniffing—scurried after the guys. Not wanting to be left on that porch by myself in case the front door came flying open, I hurried down the steps.

I didn't catch up to them until they were rounding the garage I'd fallen off of a few months earlier. There was no sign of our crazy escape attempt now. At least, there wasn't any sign that I could see. Viktor glanced back, probably to make sure I was still following, before hurrying to the back of the house. The porch at the back was smaller and had fewer steps. It was also a lot cleaner.

"This is a bad idea," I said, even though nobody was listening to me anymore. Viktor just shook his head as he approached the back door. "Look at the porch."

"What about it?"

"It's too clean."

He frowned. "Looks pretty dirty to me," he said, regarding the shoe prints stamped onto the wooden planks.

"There's no undisturbed debris," I pointed out. "This door gets used. A lot. There's probably someone in there right now, aiming their gun at the door because they heard that stupid dog—"

"We can knock, if it'll make you feel better."

"We're not going to *knock*," I said, staring at him in disbelief. It took a moment before I realized he was just teasing me. His lumpy scar twisted in a smirk as he turned back to the door and grasped the knob.

I winced. Actually, it was more than a wince. Every muscle in my body clenched in anticipation of something flying through that doorway. Bullets. Riftballs.

Some zit-faced kid who fancied himself an expert in hand-to-hand combat. But as the door creaked open, all that emerged was silence.

"Huh," Viktor said. He pushed the door a little wider. No lights appeared to be on, so the interior was pretty dark. "Not too bright."

"Who? You?"

He ignored my barb. "They should be leaving *some* lights on overnight to make it look occupied. Amateurs." Stepping across the threshold, he held up his hand as if to tell us to wait. It wasn't like I was about to go pushing past him, anyway. His boots seemed really loud on the floor, but that was probably just because everything seemed loud at that moment. Buddy's panting sounded like someone blowing into a microphone. "Come on," Viktor said at last, his voice making me jump. Click stepped into the dark house, Buddy following at his heels. I looked around the overgrown backyard, almost expecting to see someone lurking in the bushes, ready to strike. But the yard appeared to be empty. And I really didn't want to be standing on that often-used back porch when Joshua's goons came back, so I tiptoed into the house.

It smelled a little different than the last time. Fresher. Thank god. Someone had obviously done something about the body, because that awful whiff of decay I remembered wasn't there. Instead, I smelled BO, mold, and—running as a skunky undercurrent—weed.

"There better be something else in here," I muttered to myself. "If I'm going to risk my life, I want more than a dime bag."

"What?" Viktor asked, his voice so comparatively loud that I had an urge to spring forward and slap my hand across his mouth. Instead, I clamped my own mouth shut, hoping that keeping quiet would discourage him from talking altogether.

The house wasn't completely dark, but it was pretty damn shadowy, and I couldn't see much other than vague furniture shapes. I could hear more than that, though, especially since we were in the kitchen. The fridge hummed and sighed; it was probably as old as Grandpa's. I could just make out a few magnets on its dirty white surface, but anything important those magnets might have held up was long gone. Buddy's nails clicked on the vinyl floor as he sniffed his way around the room. Our feet caused that floor to give up a few plastic-sounding creaks. I tried to step a little more quietly as I followed Viktor and Click farther into the house.

The stairs were where I remembered, and Viktor was heading straight for them. I shook my head and came to a stop.

"No."

His shadow stopped and seemed to turn in my direction. "No?"

"I'm not going up there."

"You think they keep the good stuff in the kitchen?"

"They're stupid."

"Yeah . . . I don't think they're *that* stupid, Léa." He reached out and grabbed the finial on the railing, then paused. "You want to wait down here?"

"No, I don't want to wait down here and be a sitting duck."

"Then come with us."

"I don't want to have to jump off a roof again, either."

"Technically, you didn't jump off a roof. You jumped from one roof to another."

I didn't say anything.

"I feel like you're giving me a dirty look. Are you giving me a dirty look?"

"Shut up."

He chuckled and started up the stairs. Click began to follow. "No. Stay down here with Léa and keep watch. I'll make it quick."

I sighed, but I didn't argue. Neither did Click . . . although, arguing didn't seem to be something he ever did. He was probably the most agreeable guy I knew. Too bad he had such a smelly sidekick.

Two smelly sidekicks, if we were being completely accurate.

Buddy didn't seem to get the memo to stay put; he jumped up the stairs after Viktor. I let him go. He knew his way around the house, after all.

The light coming in through the windows seemed to be brightening the house a bit. Not enough that I could make out Click's features, but enough that I didn't feel quite so claustrophobic. I could see where things were, and I could see the path back to our exit. The door was still open in the kitchen, letting in the sound of intermittent birdsong. It seemed like a nice, relaxing morning.

It was too bad I couldn't enjoy it.

"He better find *something*," I said, half to myself and half to Click. "I'm tired of eating pine needles."

"Pine needles are perfectly edible," Viktor's voice said, drifting down the stairwell.

"So you say. Did you find anything?"

"Not yet. I'm going to check the attic."

"Hurry up."

"Nah . . . I think I'll take my time. Hangry Léa is super fun to hang around with."

My cheeks rushed with annoyed heat, and before I realized what I was doing, I was already stalking back to the kitchen. Now that my eyes had adjusted, I could make out more of the room, including the fact that it was a mess. There was a table, but the chairs that must've once been there were missing. Empty boxes littered the floor. At least, I assumed they were empty; I didn't know why anyone would store full boxes of food haphazardly on the floor like that. Storming to the fridge, I grabbed the handle and wrenched it open. Unsurprisingly, it was empty.

"Fuck," I muttered, tossing the door closed again. I opened up the separate door for the freezer, just in case, but the smaller compartment was clogged with ice. It looked like there might've been something in there, but it would probably require a chisel (or a sledgehammer) to get it out.

A sudden rumble caught my attention, and I froze, listening. The sky had been clear, so it wasn't thunder. The sound might've been a low-flying plane . . . but it was a lot more rhythmic than that. I backed away from the fridge and peered toward the stairs, just as the sound registered.

"Fart!" Viktor shouted, thundering down the last of the steps and flailing over the bottom few. He landed in a sprawling crouch, ducking as a splash of pink energy splattered on the wall beside him. He was on his feet a second later, barrelling toward me, pushing Click ahead of him.

"Bah-dee!" Click shouted. I shook my head and stumbled back toward the open door. The rumble was still going, coalescing into the sound of multiple heavy footsteps on the stairs.

"What happened?" I shouted. There was no point in being quiet now. Click was pushing against Viktor, probably trying to see where his dog was. But when a white streak oozed past their legs, past me, and out the door, he turned and ran. Viktor grabbed my hand and yanked me so hard that I almost lost my footing.

"Fuckers!" someone shouted, just as we exploded through the door and out into the morning. They didn't sound far behind us, and I wasn't about to look over my shoulder and check. Viktor leaped off the porch, bypassing the four steps altogether, and landed in a cat-like crouch. I wasn't quite so graceful. Even though my hand was still solidly grasped in another, I ended up doing a faceplant on the overgrown weed patch that passed for a lawn. I didn't even feel pain, despite hitting pretty hard. Viktor yanked me to my feet, and we sprinted around the side of the house.

Click and Buddy were already halfway down the block. Viktor was a step ahead of me, still tugging on my hand. I tried to pull out of his grasp, but he gripped my hand tighter.

"Let go!"

"Like heck," he said, glancing behind him. A pinging sound ricocheted through the morning, and he let out a grunt.

"What was that?" I asked, but my question was interrupted by another ping and a sharp yip from Buddy. The dog skittered to the side, still running. It took a moment for me to realize what was going on. "They're *shooting* at us?"

Viktor didn't respond to my question of disbelief. He just quickened his stride, leaving me to try to keep up and not fall flat on my face.

CHAPTER 2

DON'T LOOK BACK

Joshua's goons might've had guns, but they were also lazy. They didn't even bother to chase us down the street, opting instead to stand on the sidewalk and shoot their silly little pellets at us. By the time we were a block away, we were already out of range, so we slowed to a walk. I wrenched my hand out of Viktor's and looked up at him with a scowl as I massaged my shoulder.

"Were you *trying* to dislocate my—" My words died in my mouth as I noticed the mark on his cheekbone. "Shit."

"What?" He probed at the pink spot with his fingers. "Did it break the skin?"

"No." I shuddered anyway. "Next time, don't turn your good eye toward people who are shooting at you."

Dropping his hand, he gave me a bemused look.

"Then how am I supposed to see if they're shooting at me?"

I quickly turned away. I didn't even want to think about what might have happened if that kid's aim had been a little better—or worse.

"Hey, Click!" Viktor called. "Stop for a sec. I think Buddy might've gotten hit."

Click, who was half a block ahead of us, stopped and looked back. Buddy stopped, too, and looked up at his BFF, his scruffy tail giving an uncertain little wag. We caught up a few seconds later, and Viktor crouched down. Buddy immediately scampered out of the way.

"Grab him," Viktor said, waving his hand at the dog. Click reached down and swept him off the ground into his arms. Buddy immediately squirmed and tried to lick his face.

"I think he's fine," I said. Viktor nodded as he stood up.

"Probably. Those pellets sting, though." He reached out and ran his fingers through the fur on Buddy's hindquarters. The dog didn't seem bothered by that at all, so Viktor finished up with a scratch under the chin.

"Now what?" I asked, because nobody else seemed to be bothered by the very pressing issue at hand. Viktor turned to me with a frown.

"Now what . . . what?"

"We didn't make it to the cache we were supposed to hit."

"So we'll do it now. No big deal."

I looked down at the hand that had been clutching the scrap of paper. It was empty. "Great. Do you remember the address?"

"That was your job."

"Oh, my god. Shut up!"

He looked at me for a moment, mouth twitching.

"Do you *want* me to punch you?"

"Whoa." He held up his hands. "No need to get violent here."

"All we managed to do this morning was get shot at."

"Technically, Buddy and I *did* get shot."

My fists clenched. Click took a step closer, as if he were about to step in between us.

"Vee-kah."

"Okay. Fine. I'm sorry." He sighed and reached up to smooth back some hairs that had escaped his ponytail. "I'm hungry, too."

"Exactly. We're *all* hungry. This was our last shot with Ryver. In case you haven't noticed, she doesn't like us much."

"She likes me."

"Yeah?"

"Yeah. Everybody likes me."

"Unbelievable."

He shook his head with a smile. "I know, right? What are the chances someone would be so great that everybody likes them?"

I looked back along the sidewalk. The kids with the guns were gone. They were probably back inside the cache house. Probably eating. The fact that the place was guarded meant that there most likely *was* something to steal. And we'd had to walk away from it.

"Damn it," I mumbled.

"I bet I can cheer you up," Viktor said. My gaze snapped back to him. He raised his eyebrows. "Think I can?"

"I doubt it. Not unless you've got a steak stuffed in your pants."

"A steak? No. Well, I wouldn't call it *that*, but . . ."

"Fuck."

He laughed and reached back into his jeans pocket. The object he pulled out glinted in the sunlight. My heart sank.

"A watch?"

"An expensive watch," he clarified, angling the face to show me the logo on the dial. I shook my head.

"What good does that do us?"

"It's currency," he said, handing it to me. The metal-link band was warm, probably from being stuffed in a pocket next to his hot butt cheek. "We can trade it."

"Who's going to want a watch? Most people still have their phones. And the clocks on those still work."

"Not everybody has a phone." He raised his eyebrows in a pointed expression.

"I don't want a watch, either. The sun is good enough for me."

"What if it's cloudy?"

With a sigh, I slipped the watch onto my wrist. He helped fasten the clasp. It was obviously a men's accessory because it dwarfed my wrist and looked more like a loose bracelet than anything else. When it was as secure as it was going to get, I let my hands fall to my sides and looked up at him.

"If we're lucky, Ryver might be willing to trade. But don't count on it."

"Yeah. She might not even know how to tell time."

I gave him a look. "She's not stupid."

"Then why won't she take me up on my offer?"

"Because she's not stupid," I said, turning and heading down the sidewalk. I expected him to follow, and I wasn't wrong. Click must've put Buddy down, too, because I could hear the dog's nails on the cement.

Technically, we had no home. This job was supposed to change that. Everyone had to prove themselves in the Rift Zone. If you wanted to work for a boss—or be protected by a boss—you had to show them you were worth the risk and the hassle. Ryver Wells controlled the area in the centre of Kenyonville. There were plenty of businesses there, including the vet clinic. But the one thing her turf didn't have was a checkpoint . . . which meant that her lackeys had to be excellent thieves.

We, unfortunately, were not.

As we reached Main Street, my mind was whirling. It wasn't really getting anywhere, though; my ability to think was being severely hampered by hunger, and I couldn't think about much except our problems. Solutions danced just out of reach. I peered dazedly through windows as we passed them (there were a surprising number still intact), hoping to catch a glimpse of something we could nab. But the bakery's cases were empty and dark. The ice cream parlour was a sticky mess (and, after three years, any leftovers would've been inedible, anyway). A café with smashed-out windows seemed to have been taken over by . . . something. There was an awful lot of leaf debris and nesting material tucked into every corner. I didn't see anything alive, but that didn't mean much. Those critters were probably out searching for something to eat.

Just like we were.

"We need to do something," I said to myself. Unfortunately, I said it out loud.

"We *are* doing something," Viktor said. "Wow. You must really be hungry if you don't realize you're walking down a street."

"Can you just be serious for two seconds?"

"I can probably manage that." He counted softly under his breath, then turned to me with a grin. I looked away.

"This isn't working."

"Are you breaking up with me?"

"I'd love to. But non-psycho guys are hard to find after a magical apocalypse."

He sucked in a mock gasp. "Are we . . . You mean, we're actually a *couple?*"

"You wish."

A moan escaped him as he staggered to the side, clutching the imaginary knife in his heart. I shoved him away from me.

"You're underage, dumbass."

"I'm seventeen and a half."

"If you're still counting in halves, you're too young for me."

"Okay, then . . . I'm seventeen-point-five-seven years old."

"Uh-huh."

"You want to check my math?"

"I believe you."

CHAPTER 3

BURNING SOME BRIDGES

Viktor fell silent as we continued to walk. As the morning wore on, more people were venturing outside. Not a lot (after all, there was really nowhere to go and nothing to do other than try to scrounge up something to eat), but enough that the town centre didn't look so much like the post-apocalyptic landscape that it actually was. Click, as usual, had a spring in his step and scampered ahead of us, Buddy at his heels. Despite the fact that he'd been eating just as little as Viktor and me (less, since he was sharing with Buddy), he didn't seem to be suffering. His cheeks still had the plump of health, and when he took off his jacket, the arms underneath weren't all spindly. I couldn't really say the same for Viktor. He was starting to look a bit like a daddy-long-legs. It didn't help that he was still growing and his black t-shirt was getting tight. I was starting to see ribs.

Ryver Wells lived in a townhouse complex just a

block or so off Main Street. Back before the Rift had opened up and swallowed our lives and futures, the place had been one of those villages meant for moderately wealthy older folks. There were gates, but they seemed to be permanently closed; if you wanted in or out, you had to climb over the squat brick posts on either side. Luckily, we were all still able to do that . . . although, if I didn't get something decent to eat soon, I wasn't sure how much longer my body was going to be willing to climb.

Click went first, as usual, but not before handing Buddy to Viktor. After the dog was passed over, I went next. Viktor followed, and we headed for the clubhouse in the centre of the complex.

"Hey," Viktor said to a couple of teenage girls who were squeezed together on a ratty lounge chair in an overgrown front yard. It looked like they were probably trying to work on their tans, judging by their attire of bras and panties.

"Idiots," I muttered.

"What?" Viktor asked, turning to me as we passed the girls. "Gotta get some vitamin D."

"The sun's barely up. All they're going to do is get the horny boys all hot and bothered."

"By getting vitamin D?"

"By sitting around in their underwear, smartass."

"Huh. I didn't notice."

"Sure, you didn't."

He shrugged carelessly and cast a sideways smirk at me. "I only have eyes for—"

"If you finish that sentence, you're going to end up with a bruise."

"Right." He shook his head. "Sorry. My bad. I only have *eye* for— Ow!"

I shook out my hand, my knuckles throbbing. Punching someone who was wasting away from hunger was not a smart move.

The door to the clubhouse stood open, as it usually did during the day. The air conditioning had apparently broken during the first summer, and the place got pretty hot. I wasn't entirely sure why Ryver chose to live there and not in one of the townhouses, but I suspected it was something to do with the perception of power. Sort of like how Joshua liked to receive his subjects while sitting in a DIY recliner throne.

"Knock, knock!" Viktor said as we approached the threshold. "Everyone decent in there?"

"Come in," Ryver's voice said. Viktor strode right in, followed by Click. I approached a little more slowly, trying to figure out what we were going to tell her. I knew Viktor would probably shoot his mouth off before I could get anything out, but I still felt like we needed some sort of excuse.

The clubhouse was a sizeable building. The main area was about two storeys high, except there weren't any actual storeys. It was just an octagonal, open space with windows that encircled the upper part of the room. On one side, a wall of glass doors—also open—looked out over a patio and an empty pool.

Tables with unfurled umbrellas were scattered over the cement deck. It was too bad there were no chairs to go with them; sitting in the shade might've made a nice change.

A neatly made bed sat opposite the glass doors. It would've had a nice view out over the pool . . . if the pool had been anything to look at. A few deputies stood around, arms folded, expressions dour. When we entered the room, they glanced at us, then turned their attention back to the woman sitting on the bed.

Ryver Wells was one of the older female Rifters in Kenyonville . . . which meant that she was around twenty-two. She didn't seem to leave her place much, which made her full face of sun-kissed freckles kind of a mystery. It was probably just genetics. Along with the freckles, she had a mass of curly red hair that didn't seem to want to be tamed. Even now, with most of her hair pulled and twisted back with a fabric headband, myriad wild tendrils still danced around her head. As she turned to look at us, those strands waved like snakes, making me think of Medusa. The cold look she gave us certainly didn't help.

"Well?" she said, looking straight at me. I shrivelled under her intense gaze. I'd never been close enough to determine her actual eye colour. They were probably hazel . . . but in certain lighting, they almost looked yellow.

"No food," Viktor said, jumping in before I could even open my mouth.

"Not possible. We've been scouting that place for months."

Viktor reached back and tightened his ponytail. It was something he often did when he was nervous. Maybe Ryver's gaze was getting to him, too. "Well, we didn't actually make it to that cache."

One of the deputies, a guy around my age named Howell, snorted. "Told you they'd be useless."

Ryver shook her head, still staring at Viktor. "So where have you been?"

"We found something better." He grabbed my arm and hauled me closer. His agile fingers unclasped the watch and slipped it from my wrist. "You can trade it for something. For a *lot* of somethings."

Ryver frowned as she took the offered watch and turned it over in her hands, giving it a good examination. "Where'd you get this?"

"A cache house. Just not the one you sent us to."

Her lips pulled into a little pucker, and she looked up at Viktor. "Are you serious?"

I could almost feel the self-assuredness drain out of the guy standing next to me. He shook his head. "What?"

"What am I supposed to do with a fucking watch?"

"Trade it."

"Trade it with who? The guy you stole it from?" She shook her head and held up the timepiece. "Is this Joshua's?"

"Heck if I know. I just found it."

"In a cache house."

"Yeah."

"Whose?"

"Joshua's. But that doesn't mean it was his."

"That's exactly what it means, Viktor." She let out a disgusted grunt and tossed the watch to Howell. "It was in his cache, so it either belonged to him or he stole it from someone else. Either way—"

"Rift Zone rules. Finders keepers."

"So you keep it," she said, waving her hand at Howell, who held the watch out to us. "And good luck getting anything for it."

Viktor frowned, but he said nothing as he took back the watch and slipped it into his pocket. Ryver was still staring at us, her yellow gaze appraising.

"Why didn't you go where I sent you?"

"Long story," he said.

"Fine." She shook her head and waved her hand. "Give me the short version."

"We were at this other cache first, so we thought we'd check it out while we were there."

"And why didn't you go to the address I gave you?"

"We forgot it."

The suddenness of Viktor's answer seemed to bring her up short. She sat up a little straighter, her eyebrows rising in disbelief. "You *forgot* it? I wrote it down for you."

"Yeah. About that. We sort of lost—"

"Are you kidding me?" Her eyes seemed to flash. I

took a sliding step backward. "So that piece of paper is out there, just floating around?"

"Yeah," Viktor said slowly. He obviously wasn't sure what Ryver was getting at. Neither was I, to be honest.

"Unbelievable. We spent *months* casing that place. Joshua didn't know we knew about it. But now, thanks to you three morons, he will."

"He might not find the paper."

"Where do you think you lost it?"

He chewed his lip for a moment. "The cache. But—"

"Get out."

Viktor jerked like he'd been slapped. "What?"

"Get out." She jabbed her finger toward the front door. Her deputies were turned toward us, too, flanking their leader like a trio of bodyguards. They didn't carry guns like Joshua's goons did, but still.

"Wait a minute," Viktor said. "One mistake and you're just going to—"

"You told me you could handle it. But all you did was fuck up a supply line that we've been working on for months." She jabbed her finger again. This time, the digit flared pink. I took another step back and grabbed Viktor's arm.

"Let's go," I whispered. But he didn't move.

"That's not fair," he said. "Why do *we* have to jump through so many hoops just to get a few mouthfuls? This place is crawling with kids who are sitting around working on their tans!"

"They're just kids. I don't expect them to risk their necks. It's our responsibility to make sure they stay alive until all of this is over."

"It'll never be over if you have anything to say about it."

Ryver's eyes widened. "What's *that* supposed to mean?"

"We could get all of them out tomorrow. Well, not tomorrow. But soon. If you'd just let me—"

"Your plan is bullshit, Viktor, and you know it. Stop messing with the poor kids. You think the military is just going to let them walk out of here?"

"They let *us* out."

She shook her head. "Sorry. I don't believe you. No person in their right mind would come back to this if they'd somehow managed to get out."

"He's not in his right mind," I muttered. She glanced at me, frowning.

"You're not kidding."

"Fart!" Viktor said, taking a step toward the bed. But all that happened was that Ryver's hand opened up and we got a really good view of the Rift energy running over it.

"Find another boss to screw over," she said. "And don't even think of trying to convince any of my kids to try to get out of here. All you'll do is put them in danger, not least because they'd have to cross through some other boss' turf."

"You're not their mom."

"I'm the best they've got." She shook the pink from her hand and nodded at Howell, who stepped forward. I skittered back toward the door. But Viktor just stood there, glaring.

"Your best is *spit*," he said. "At least I'm doing something other than sitting around and waiting."

"And how's that working out for you?"

Viktor clenched his fists, but he didn't say anything else. He turned on his heel and stalked out the open door, not even bothering to wait for me or Click.

CHAPTER 4

PLAN B

I hated to admit it, but Ryver had a point. About a few things.

We had screwed up. No, *I* had screwed up by losing the address. I'd had it in my hand at the cache house, and then I hadn't. So I'd probably dropped it during our escape.

The watch probably wasn't as great of a find as Viktor thought it was. In fact, it was probably a liability. If any of Joshua's goons saw it on one of us, they'd know exactly where we'd gotten it. So we couldn't trade it in his part of town.

Not that we were exactly welcome there, anyway. Not after the debacle that had led to Buddy almost getting eaten. I *had* thrown a Riftball at the little pissant's throne, after all.

But there was the biggest point that Ryver was right about: We'd come back. If we were keeping track and ranking the stupidest decisions that were made by Rifters, that was probably at the top of the list. Of course, we hadn't known we were going to be homeless; we'd thought we could just go back to Viktor and Click's house and resume our pre-escape lives.

But that plan had gone out the window.

By unspoken agreement, we headed north, back toward Niesha's turf. We might not have been welcome in our old house, but we were at least fairly safe. I knew Viktor was probably thinking about the pine trees in that area of town. (If I had to choke down any more needles, though, I was going to scream.)

We passed the park where we'd met up after our first expedition together, after I'd jumped off a roof and twisted my ankle. It was fairly busy, with more than a few toddlers screaming and running around. The demographics of Kenyonville were weird. Aside from a small handful of adults who'd applied to stay, almost everyone else was under the age of twenty-five. There was a gap where we were missing tweens and elementary school-age kids. Then there were toddlers and babies, offspring of the older Rifters who'd been stupid enough to procreate in a post-apocalyptic prison. There was also the gender imbalance; because of the way the Rift affected people at puberty, there were more female than male Rifters on the younger end of the age group and the opposite on the older end. It all would've made for an interesting study . . . though nobody on the outside seemed inclined to pay attention to us at all.

The park's noise gradually drifted away as we walked, and the sounds were replaced with birdsong. I even heard a lawnmower at one point. Electric, of course (unless someone had been rationing gas . . . but there were better things to do with that fuel than try to improve curb appeal).

"Viktor."

"Yeah?"

"What happened to Niesha's lawnmower?"

He snorted and looked down at me. "What?"

"She kept it in a shed, right?"

"Yeah. Out back."

"It didn't burn with the rest of the house, though."

"The shed? No. Why?"

I shrugged. "It's shelter."

"It's also locked." He'd long since taken his jacket off. When he transferred it to his other hand, the movement reminded me that I was getting a little warm. I pulled off my own jacket and tied the sleeves around my waist. "We can go have a look if you want," he said.

I nodded, my throat tight.

"Still not sleeping?"

"I don't know how you and Click do it. I just feel so exposed."

He sighed. "I don't sleep *well.*"

I came to a stop. He frowned back at me as he took a few more steps, but then he stopped, too.

"What?"

"I want you to do something."

"Oh, goody! A quest." He stepped closer, sort of bouncing on the balls of his feet. Click stopped beside us, looking puzzled.

"Hardly." I looked up at Viktor, just as he turned and peered down the sidewalk. "Look at me."

"Okay." He turned back and fixed me with a solemn stare. His cheeks seemed to be looking a little more gaunt. I fixed my gaze on his dark eye and took a deep breath.

"I want you and Click—"

"Yeah . . ."

"—to take Buddy—"

"Yeah . . ."

"—and go make nice with Katja."

"No."

"Viktor, come on! Why should all three of us starve and shiver?"

"Who's shivering?" He lifted his arms, showing off the dark stains on his t-shirt.

"You're too skinny."

"Maybe I should become a runway model." He strutted away a few steps, then turned dramatically, his ponytail whipping as he swung around.

"Are you done?"

"No . . . but my modelling career probably is."

I let out a deep sigh. "You and Click should go. There's no reason we should all be homeless and hungry."

"Um, yeah, there is."

"What?"

"We're a team." He looked at Click. "Right?"

Click gave him a thumbs up. I shook my head.

"We're not a team."

"Kind of seems like we are."

"I only met you guys a few months ago. If we go back to the way things were, I can take care of myself."

"Is that what you want?"

No, I want to be out of this stupid prison, I thought. But I didn't let the words escape.

"I made you come back," he said. His words hit me almost like a blow, and I took a step back as I looked up into his face. The sad expression he wore was one I'd only seen a few times. It didn't suit him.

"I didn't *have* to follow you back in here."

"Then why did you?"

I shrugged. His mouth twitched.

"'Cause we're a team?"

"Shut up. Maybe I just didn't trust that you wouldn't do something stupid." I tugged on the jacket sleeves tied around my waist. "And if anyone should be blaming themselves for the mess we're in, it's me."

He blinked. "Why?"

"Because I'm the reason we're homeless."

"No, jealous donkeybutts are the reason we're homeless." He frowned as he stepped a little closer. "Do you expect me to blame you because Niesha may or may not have had a crush on someone? How the heck is that *your* fault?"

"If I weren't with you, you could go back."

"Well, you *are* with us. And I don't want to go grovelling to a bunny like that." Before I could think of a comeback, he turned away and started down the sidewalk. Click and Buddy scampered after him.

—

We hadn't been back to Niesha's house since the morning of the fire. The surrounding laneways looked the same, and when we approached the gate in the fence, I noticed that it was still open, probably the way Niesha had left it when she'd stormed out of the yard. I really couldn't see much past the fence until we got closer and I could peer through the opening. As we stepped into the overgrown backyard, Viktor heaved a sigh.

"What a farting mess."

"What did you expect?" I asked, peering at the ruins. There really wasn't much left. Some charred wood. A blackened foundation. It was a wonder the ornamental shrubbery hadn't burned.

"Think there's anything to salvage?"

"I doubt it. Besides, Niesha would've looked for anything that might have survived." My attention was drawn to Buddy, who'd found a stick in the long grass. He brought it over to Click, dropped it at his feet, then jumped back, tail wagging. I turned around and spotted the shed. "It's still here."

"It's still locked," Viktor pointed out. He strode over to it and grasped the doorknob. I expected to hear a rattle as the movement came up against the lock. But, to my surprise—and probably his as well— the knob turned. I hurried closer.

"Open it," I said, because he was just standing there, knob turned, not moving. He looked at me with a frown.

"Niesha always kept this locked," he said, keeping his voice low. "So if it's not . . ."

He didn't have to finish the thought. My throat tightened, and I had a sudden urge to let out a scream of frustration. Or kick the fence. But I managed to clamp down on it.

Viktor bit his lip for a moment as he stared at the knob, and I got the distinct impression that he was psyching himself up for something. I wasn't sure what he expected to find on the other side of that door.

I wasn't sure I wanted to know.

"Okay," he whispered. He flexed the fingers of his free hand and blew an infinitesimal raspberry.

"Seriously?" I hissed.

"Sorry. Force of habit." He held the pink glow carefully out to the side and braced his feet. I took a step back, edging toward the still-open gate, ready to run if I needed to. He slowly pushed the door open.

Nothing happened. There was no sound. Nothing came flying out at us. Viktor grunted and waved his pink-glowing hand inside the dark space.

"Spit!" he shouted, and flailed backward. My body reacted, sprinting for the gate before my mind even knew what it was doing.

"What?" I shouted, not daring to look behind me. "What?"

I was halfway down the lane when I heard the laughter. Adrenaline still surging, I spun on my heel and marched back to the gate, through it, and up to Viktor, whose one dark eye was dancing with merriment that matched the wide grin on his face. The punch thudded through the air.

"Lee-ah," Click said, sounding way too much like a chiding parent. Viktor rubbed his shoulder, a bemused smile on his face.

"Yeah, Léa. Why so punchy?"

"Shut. Up. What is *wrong* with you?"

"Well, you see, I got stuck in this post-apocalyptic heckhole with this hangry girl who keeps hitting me. Can't she see I'm *fragile*?"

"You're not fragile," I spat. "You're an asshole." Tears sprang to my eyes. I wanted to punch him again, but I no longer felt like I had the energy.

"Hey. It's fine. I'm sorry." He stepped toward me. I held out my hand to block him, but he just stepped forward until it was pressed against his chest. "I'm sorry, okay?"

"Go to Katja's!" I wailed. "Just go! If not for yourself, then for me."

He frowned. "How will that help you?"

I shook my head and looked away, letting my hand fall. Only two steps separated us, and the next thing I knew, I was wrapped in a hug. I didn't have the energy to fight it; I was too busy trying to swallow the tears down my aching throat.

"Maybe hunger is making you forget," he said, his voice rumbling against my ear, "so I'll just have to keep reminding you. We're a team. So we're not going anywhere without you. Okay?"

"No." My voice was tiny and miserable. He chuckled softly.

"You're all right."

I closed my eyes. I wanted so much to believe him. But things had sucked since we'd walked back into the Rift Zone over a month earlier. We were sleeping on the hard ground, eating pine needles and the few berries we knew weren't poisonous, and all of us were slowly losing our life force. I didn't even have to try that hard to ground the Rift energy when I got startled or angry; my body seemed to be redirecting resources elsewhere.

"There's a whole town of Rifters who've figured it out," he said, keeping his voice low and soothing. "We've just had it too good for too long, and now we don't know what to do. But we'll figure it out, too."

I pushed away, leaving him with his arms sort of hanging in a quasi-hug position.

"What?" he asked.

"You stink too much for prolonged hugs."

He let out a grunt of laughter as he dropped his arms.

"*How* will we figure this out?" I asked, grabbing my jacket sleeves and giving them a tug.

"Good thing you have me with you." He laced his long fingers together and pressed his hands outward, cracking a few knuckles. "First, we get clear on our priorities."

"Food."

"Right."

"If I have to eat another tree, I'm going to scream."

He nodded. "Maybe we *should* hit up Katja."

I gaped at him. "You *just* said—"

"Not without you. And we're not looking for a place to live. But we know she's got a network of cache houses."

"You want to steal from her?"

"As a last resort."

"And what's the first resort?"

He reached up and tucked a loose strand of hair behind his ear. "I'll use my considerable charms and—"

I interrupted him with a snort. "We need to be realistic."

"I am!" He pressed a hand to his chest, looking offended. I rolled my eyes. "She's not a monster, Léa. If I ask nicely, she might give us something. If not, maybe she's got a job we can do."

"A job *you* can do," I corrected him. "If she knows I'm involved, she might not want to help at all."

"Okay. I won't mention you, then. But if this works, we might be able to get *something* to eat."

"And if it doesn't work?"

He shrugged. "I know where most of the cache houses are. We'll just have to have ourselves a little raid."

That doesn't sound like a terrible plan at all, I thought. But I kept it to myself.

It wasn't like we had any other good options.

CHAPTER 5

AFTER THE COUP

The lawnmower was gone. We found that out when we checked the shed before leaving. All that was in the windowless space were a few spiders . . . which killed my desire to sleep in there pretty quick.

After closing up the empty shed (which was pretty pointless), we headed over to Katja's house. The sun was high overhead and felt too warm on my arms. Click still had that inexplicable spring in his step, which I found both fascinating and annoying. And he didn't seem that bothered by the temperature; he kept his denim jacket on over his fancy shirt. I felt unbearably hot just looking at him.

"Think that's Niesha's?" Viktor asked as we turned the corner onto Katja's street. I blinked, half dazed by heat and hunger.

"Huh?"

"Listen."

I did. The familiar buzz of an electric lawnmower pierced through the haze. "Who would want to mow on a day like this?"

"Maybe they have an air-conditioned house to go back into when they're done."

I shot him a dirty look.

"I'm just saying." He jerked his chin, pointing down the sidewalk. "We're almost there. Maybe you should wait here."

"Take Click," I said. "And Buddy. If she has a heart, she's not going to make a dog go hungry."

He came to a stop and looked down at me, a thoughtful expression on his face. "You going to be here when we get back?"

"Why wouldn't I be?"

He shrugged. "You might run away."

I said nothing. The thought *had* crossed my mind.

"Okay. Click's staying with you."

"No, he's not," I said, just as Click gave a thumbs up. I put my hand on his, pushing it back down. "I'm not going to run away like a feral dog."

"You might run away like you're trying to be this noble, self-sacrificing hero." He shook his head. "There's no guarantee we wouldn't have ended up in this position if you hadn't been there."

"Her lackey said—"

"I don't put much stock in what donkeybutts say."

I let out a sigh. "Fine. Just hurry up. Even if we

do score something to eat, we still need to find a place to crash for the night. I'm tired of sleeping under the stars, no matter how pretty you keep saying they are."

He opened his mouth to say something, then seemed to think better of it. It was just as well.

Glancing at Click, he turned and loped down the street, swinging his jacket at his side. His easy stride was all for show; he'd been dragging a bit, just like me. But it was best not to show any sort of weakness, including your level of hunger. That was the sort of thing that could be used for leverage to get you to do really stupid things.

Like break into a cache house inhabited by two stinky boys.

Okay, so Click wasn't bad. I was starting to think that he wasn't even human. Despite the heat, he didn't seem to be sweating. I couldn't really smell anything unless he got really close . . . and, even then, the scent was more earthy than armpitty.

I looked down at Buddy, who'd found a nice shady spot beside a vandalized community mailbox. His tongue lolled and bounced as he panted, and he looked up at Click with a squint. "He could probably use some water."

Click gave me a thumbs up and strode into the nearest yard. My heart leapt into my throat as I frantically looked to the front door. The last thing I wanted to see was a pink ticket. But the door was open, and half off its hinges. It wasn't a natural-looking sort of damage, the kind that came with normal wear and tear. Some idiot had probably been swinging on it.

What else would you expect, though, in a town populated entirely by people whose brains were in that weird phase of development where the worst ideas seemed like brilliant brainstorms?

The hose—if there had been one—was long gone, but the spigot and tap were still there. Click turned it on, allowing a gush of water to splash onto the ground. He cupped his hands under the flow.

"Bah-dee!"

The dog walked through the overgrown yard, following the sound of his BFF's voice. A moment later, all I could hear was the sound of dog tongue on liquid. For some reason, it made me have to pee . . . even though I was parched.

When Buddy had drunk his fill, Click brought the rest of the water to his mouth and slurped it up. Then he filled his hands again and turned to me.

"I'll get my own, thanks."

He grinned and drank what was in his hands. I stepped closer and crouched down, bringing my hands under the flow. The water was finger-achingly cold. I drank as much as I could, not worrying about staying dry; the dribbles down the front of my shirt actually felt nice.

"You good?" I asked when I'd had as much as I

dared. Click gave me another thumbs up, so I turned off the tap. The yard was once again plunged into near silence. Buddy wandered closer to Click and scratched at his leg. "He must be hungry," I observed. "We better find something for him to eat before he eats one of our faces."

"Lee-ah," Click said, in a way that made me sure he'd perfectly understood my words.

"It's Lay-uh."

"Lee-ah," he said again, punctuating my butchered name with a familiar throat click.

"Lay . . ."

"Lee . . ."

I sighed. "Never mind. You wouldn't be the first person to pronounce it wrong, anyway." Settling myself on the ground, I leaned back on my hands. We were in the shade, and I didn't particularly want to move. "What kind of language only has two vowel sounds?"

He just blinked at me. Even in the shadows, his golden eyes almost seemed to glow.

My body was so close to the ground that it beckoned like a magnet. I had no idea how long Viktor was going to be, though I doubted it would be more than a few minutes. All he had to do was get an answer. And, hopefully, some food. Slowly, I settled myself down on my side on the scratchy grass. It was in the shade at that moment, but its condition let me know that it was probably in direct sunlight at some point during the day. *Doesn't matter*, I thought. *I'm just closing my eyes for a sec. And I'm sure Viktor will wake me up with some stupid quip when he gets back.*

—

awoke, sweating. When I opened my eyes, only to find that I was staring at a shady patch a couple of feet away, I felt a rush of hot anger . . . which only made me feel worse. My exposed elbow was uncomfortably warm. I pushed myself up and looked around, spotting Viktor a few feet away, folded onto the grass in the shade like a spider trying to make itself more compact.

"Have a good nap?" he asked. I wanted to glare at him, but my gaze was drawn to the person sitting at his side. I frowned in confusion.

"What's going on?" I asked, rubbing my hand over my elbow. The skin felt hot. When I looked, I noticed the pink. "Damn it, Viktor. Why didn't you wake me sooner?"

"I thought you needed the sleep."

"I didn't need the sunburn, thanks." With a sigh, I turned my attention back to the people sitting in front of me. "So?"

"Oh. Yeah." He gestured to one side. "Katja's going to join us."

I squeezed my eyes shut for a moment. "How long was I asleep?" I muttered. Viktor grunted in amusement. I opened my eyes to give him a look. "You'll need to explain better than that."

"Okay . . ." He turned to Katja, who looked a little rough compared to the last time I'd seen her. The turquoise strip in her hair had faded away, leaving that piece looking slightly greenish. She didn't seem to be wasting away like Viktor and I were, but there was still a hungry look in her eyes. She sighed as Viktor hesitated.

"I'm out," she said.

"Out?" I repeated. "What does that mean?"

"There was a coup," Viktor said. "The Pinkball Rebellion."

Katja turned to him in disbelief. "The *what?*"

"He need to come with his own glossary," I said. "You'll get used to it."

She shook her head. "I *told* Niesha this would happen."

"What did happen?" I asked. She shook her head and stared down at her hands in her lap.

"Xavi. I didn't even last a week."

I frowned. "Isn't he, like, fifteen?"

She nodded, picking at a loose thread on her shorts.

"Oh, that's just great," I muttered. "Just what we need. Another little boy running a territory."

"I should've tried harder," she said, moving her fidgeting from the thread to the greenish strand of hair. "Niesha was in such a rush to get out of here that she didn't make her wishes known. Properly." She nodded in my direction. "You remember. You were there."

I nodded. "Did you tell the others when you saw them?"

"I told Draven first. I think he's the only one who believed me. Crystal took Xavi's side. So when Xavi evicted me—"

"He *evicted* you? How the hell do you get evicted by a fifteen-year-old pissant?"

In answer, she raised her hand. Pink tendrils of energy swirled up from her fingertips. I clamped my mouth shut.

"I stayed in the area. Draven smuggled me some food for a couple of weeks. But Xavi caught him and threatened to kick him out, too, if he kept it up. So Draven made his choice . . . and here I am." She shook the pink from her hand with a dismissive gesture.

"I told her she could come with us," Viktor said.

"Because we're just rolling in food and luxury accommodations?" I asked, turning back to Katja. Despite being able to relate to her predicament, I was having a hard time mustering up much sympathy. "Do you even *want* to go with us?"

She frowned. "It's not like I have much of a choice."

"Yeah, but I come as part of the package. If you have a problem with that—"

"A problem?" she repeated. She looked genuinely confused.

"We wouldn't be homeless, either, if it wasn't for you."

Her puzzled expression deepened. She turned to Viktor for an explanation.

"One of your lackeys banished us."

"Why?"

He waved his hand in my direction. "Apparently, you hate Léa for taking Niesha out of the Zone."

"Leaving was Niesha's idea," I added, drawing Katja's attention back to me. "I didn't force her to do anything. So if you have a problem with that . . . this isn't going to work."

She held up her hands. "Wait. Who told you I had a problem?"

"Crystal," Viktor said. "Right after she moved into our old place. She better not scratch my DVDs."

Katja sighed. "I knew that little bitch was going to be trouble."

"So you *didn't* have a thing for Niesha?" he asked, at which Katja's cheeks went pink. I could see that, even though she was sitting in the shade.

"Doesn't really matter now, does it? I'll probably never see her again."

"Never say never. We can teach you how to get out."

She shook her head. "It won't work."

"It worked for us."

"Yeah . . . You're not telling me the whole story, Viktor."

"Sure, I am. We got out. I didn't like what I saw, so I came back."

"Uh-huh."

"We had a nice thing going here in the Zone. Comfy beds, plenty of video games and movies, a supply of Cheeznudles—"

"Oh, my god. If I have to choke down another one of those damn things, I'm going to scream."

"Well, you don't have to worry about that. We haven't seen a Cheeznudle in weeks." He reached back to tighten his ponytail, then glanced up at something behind me. I turned to find Click bouncing into the yard, Buddy at his heels. "You guys all peed out?"

Click gave him a thumbs up before striding into the shade and sitting down. His skirt sort of flared out like a flower as he sat. For some reason, that made me think of the little plaque beside Viktor's aunt and uncle's front door, the one with the sunflowers painted on it.

"I'm serious, though," Viktor said, turning back to Katja. "We've still got work to do here. Rifters need to know that they don't have to be stuck in the Zone forever. Once they get away from the Rift . . . they're cured."

She snorted. "Cured?"

"Pretty much. When we were out there, we couldn't play with pinkballs if we tried." Judging by the wicked smile starting at the corner of his mouth, he knew exactly how that sentence sounded. I rolled my eyes.

"So why is everyone still stuck in here?"

"Because nobody believes him," I said. "Either that,

or the bosses don't want to give up their power. Some of them like calling the shots."

She didn't say anything. I wasn't sure if that comment had stepped over some sort of line, but I was too tired and hungry to really care.

"Bosses are a necessary evil, though," Viktor said. He reached out and scratched Buddy's head as the dog passed him. "We should ally ourselves with one."

"Who did you have in mind?" she asked. "King Joshua? Permanent Marc?"

He snorted. "You want to go work for Permanent Marc?"

"No."

"Good. You'd look stupid with those devil bites on your forehead."

I shuddered at the thought. I hadn't actually seen any of Permanent Marc's devotees, since they stuck to his territory (and that was one place we avoided if at all possible), but there were rumours about the loyalty pledge they had to take. It involved a scarification ritual that burned two spots onto the forehead, right where devil horns would've been.

"And I don't particularly want to ruin the look I've got going," Viktor added, causing me to turn to him with a raised eyebrow. "What? You don't like the asymmetry?" He framed his face with both hands. I looked away.

"If not those two," Katja said, "that doesn't leave us many options. There's Ryver Wells—"

"Been there, done that, stole a watch, and burned a bridge," Viktor said. Katja just blinked at him.

"Okay . . . C-Roy?"

I shook my head. "Only as a last resort."

"Why?"

"Last time I worked for him, I lost a toe."

She chewed on her lip for a moment. Viktor shook his head.

"You ever going to tell us the story?"

"I just did."

"That's not a story, Léa. That's a summary. And a pretty spitty one at that."

"Spitty?" Katja said.

"Check the glossary," I muttered. I turned back to Viktor. "It was a job gone wrong, okay? I don't want to talk about it."

His gaze drifted down to my right foot, safely encased in its sneaker. I cleared my throat.

"The only other bosses are Xavi—"

"Not an option," Katja said.

"I know. I'm just saying. Beyond that . . ."

"Rasputin," Viktor said, pitching his voice a little deeper. "The most mysterious of them all."

"They've got the biggest territory in the whole town," Katja added.

"There's not much in it."

"There's a checkpoint. Which means they've got food."

My stomach, which had been fairly quiet, let out a huge growl. Viktor grunted in amusement.

"Léa's stomach is game. I guess that settles it." He looked at Click, then at Katja, before turning back to me. "Rasputin it is. But . . ."

"But what?" I asked.

He squinted up into the sky. "Their territory is on the other side of town. It's getting late. And even once we get there, we still have to find their . . . uh, lair."

"Any boss worth their salt has a proper house," Katja said.

"Joshua has a cell phone boutique."

She smirked. "My point stands."

CHAPTER 6

DESSERT FIRST

Everything looked like food when you were hungry.

As we made our way toward Rasputin's territory, heading in a vague southwesterly direction, I found myself contemplating eating things I never would've considered before. The crisped-up leaves of a neglected rosebush. The crop of dandelions in an overgrown front yard. A fencepost that looked a bit rotten and therefore chewable. Of course, some of those things *were* edible (though maybe not the fencepost), but I didn't bother telling the group to stop. Viktor seemed to have his heart set on something else.

"We could try hitting up the vet," he said as we made our way back through Ryver's territory, walking down Main Street once more. He glanced at me to gauge my reaction. I shook my head.

"You think he has food to spare?" I asked.

"He's just one old guy."

"Yeah, and there are four of us."

"Five," Katja said, pointing at Buddy, who was trotting along beside her. He looked up at the sound of her voice. The way he was panting, it almost looked like he was smiling at her. Viktor chuckled.

"Somebody has a crush." He snapped his fingers. "Hey, Buddy! Remember who keeps you fed."

"Not us," I muttered, glancing over at Click. But if he was jealous about his furry little friend's infatuation, he didn't show it.

"I used to have a dog," Katja said, seeming not to have heard me. "Schnitzel."

Viktor shot her a bemused look. I braced myself for whatever was going to come out of his mouth next. But, to my surprise, he kept it shut.

"He went with my parents," Katja went on. She kept her gaze on the ground in front of her as she walked. A tiny smile crossed her lips. It could've been because of a memory. Or maybe it was just relief. She probably knew what had happened to a lot of the pets in town.

"What was his name?" I asked. She shot me a funny look.

"Schnitzel."

Oh. Right. Cheeks burning, I looked away.

"We have to eat something soon," Viktor said. "Léa's brain is malfunctioning."

I didn't have the energy to contradict him. Besides, he wasn't wrong.

"What have you guys been eating?" Katja asked. "If not Cheeznudles—"

"Trees," I muttered.

She grunted. "Trees?"

"What's wrong with trees?" Viktor asked. "Add a few berries and . . . voilà." He made a little chef's kiss with his fingertips. "A delicious salad."

"You've found berries?"

"You haven't?"

She shook her head. "I have no idea what's not poisonous."

"Neither do I, beyond blackberries. Or anything that looks like a blackberry. Anything with drupelets is safe. There aren't any poisonous berries in that family."

"Drupelets?"

"He's some sort of genius," I said.

"Right . . ."

Viktor let out a grunt of laughter. "That sounded awfully skeptical."

"That's because you seem awfully stupid."

"Hey!"

I tried not to smile too hard. I just kept my gaze on the sidewalk in front of us and kept walking, trying to placate my aching stomach with the promise of a bit of actual food.

I hadn't been south of Ryver's townhouse complex since the Rift. C-Roy's territory was in the south, too, but on the eastern side of Kenyonville. The west, overall, tended to be a place to avoid. The northwestern quarter, where we'd made our exit earlier that summer, was under the control of Permanent Marc. Just south of that was Joshua's turf. Knowing what I knew about the guy, it seemed incredible that he would've held on to as much territory as he had, and for so long, especially being wedged between such powerful bosses. Mind you, he wasn't smart enough to be much of a threat; Permanent Marc and Rasputin probably figured trying to take over his turf would be more trouble than it was worth. Or maybe they simply wanted a buffer.

The sun was heading toward the horizon, dragging some of the heat with it, but there was still plenty of light. And we were going to need it; foraging in the dark was a great way to get scratched and punctured. Blackberry bushes were especially nasty. They seemed to enjoy attacking hungry people. That didn't deter most of us, though, and we spotted a crop easily when we came upon the crowd of half a dozen kids pushing their way into the prickly foliage that spilled over a barely visible chainlink fence. Most were wearing jackets as armour, even though the day was still warm. With a sigh, I pulled my own jacket from around my waist and slipped my arms into the sleeves. Almost immediately, I was unbearably hot.

"Come on," Viktor said, shaking his head and leading us past the group of kids who were hungrily shoving the dark berries into their mouths with stained fingers. I hesitated for a moment, staring at the sight, and my stomach let out a growl. Katja, Click, and Buddy were all still following Viktor . . . away from the food.

"No. I need to stop."

Viktor glanced back at me, then came to a halt. A frown creased his sweaty brow. "Gotta pee?"

"No, I don't have to pee. Shut up." I waved my hands at the berry bushes. "Since when do we just walk past food?"

"You want to elbow your way in?"

"There's enough for everyone."

"Berries are mostly water. Pine needles have more nutrition." He jerked his thumb over his shoulder. "I see a few promising—"

"Viktor, I swear to god, if I have to eat any part of a tree today, another part of a tree is going to get shoved up your ass."

Katja snorted and came to a stop. She didn't turn around, though, which was just as well. I knew she was laughing, and I really wasn't in the mood. Click had already stopped and was looking at me with a confused expression.

"Pinecone?" Viktor said, his voice hesitant. "I mean . . . that's kind of kinky, Léa."

I glared at him so hard it kind of hurt.

"Okay. Sorry." He held up his hands. "We can have berries if you want. Just don't come crying to me when you get all scratched up."

"When have I ever come crying to you about anything? I can take care of myself, Viktor. So stop acting like you're my father and let me fucking eat something. Okay?"

He nodded, pressing his lips together so hard that his scar crinkled. Turning back to the bushes, he sighed and shook out his jacket before sliding his skinny arms into the sleeves.

The bushes were pretty picked over, and there weren't many berries that I could reach. Luckily, we had Viktor, who snagged plenty from the upper canes and handed them down to us like some weird-ass mother bird. I noticed he gave me more than he gave to either Katja or Click, but I wasn't about to say anything. I hated the person hunger had turned me into. If eating more than my share was going to keep her at bay, then that was what I was going to do. At least until we found a more reliable source of food.

As Viktor had to stretch higher and higher, the sun got lower and the day started to cool. The other kids, having exhausted the patches of bush they could reach, wandered away one by one without saying a word to each other. We were still in Ryver's territory, but if the kids were resorting to a few berries, they probably weren't living at the complex. I wondered where they *were* living, and if they might've had room for a few more people. But then I reminded myself that they were just as hungry as we were. Rasputin was probably our best bet.

Viktor leaned so far into the bushes that I grabbed the back of his waistband to keep him from toppling into the leaves and disappearing. I had this strange, irrational fear that he would be swallowed up, disappearing from our reality entirely. He grunted and snagged a few more berries with both hands.

"Thanks," he said, still leaning at a ridiculous angle. "Mind reeling me back in now?"

I pulled back, tilting him onto his feet. I wasn't sure why he wasn't using his hands to help himself until I saw what was in them. Both were nearly full with half-crushed blackberries, their dark juice glistening in the fading light. I was tempted to just grab them and shove them into my mouth, but when I looked up at his face, I noticed the sharpness of his jaw. I took a step back.

"Full?"

I shook my head. "You eat them."

He raised his eyebrows. I raised mine right back. He turned to Click and Katja.

"She's right," Katja said. "I'm fine. I've still got seeds stuck in my teeth from what I ate."

"Click?" He held the handfuls out to the boy, who hesitated for only a moment before taking a few berries carefully in his hand. He crushed them with his fingers, causing dark juice to drip over the digits, and crouched down.

"Bah-dee," he said softly. The dog, who'd flopped down in the shade to wait until we were done with our meagre dinner, got up and trotted over. He sniffed Click's hand, then gave the juice a tentative lick. Seeming to realize that berries were the only thing being offered, he reluctantly gobbled down the mushy fruit.

"By this time tomorrow," Viktor said, popping a few berries into his mouth, "we'll have some *real* food in our stomachs."

I shook my head. "Don't bet on it."

"Somebody has to." He nudged my shoulder with the back of his hand. I glared at the smear of juice he left on my jacket.

"I'm just saying. Don't get your hopes up."

"Hope's all we've got, Léa." He held one handful of berries out to me. I shook my head again. "Come on. I don't want you yelling at me all the way to Rasputin's place."

"Why would I yell?"

"You might still be hangry."

"I—" I began, only to be interrupted by my stomach. "Shut up," I said, staring down at it. "I just fed you."

Viktor chuckled. "I don't want your stomach yelling at me, either." He gave his hand a little jerk in my direction. With a sigh, I held out my hands, cupping them into a bowl, and let him dump the berries in.

"Thanks."

"You're welcome," he said brightly, and tossed back the berries in his other hand. Chewing thoughtfully, he stared at me. I shrank back into myself.

"What?"

"You're looking better already."

"So I looked awful before?"

"Well, you didn't look great. But who am I to judge based on appearances?"

My stomach suddenly felt like someone had dumped a bowl full of ice water into it. I regarded the berries in my hands with a frown.

"We should get going," Katja said. I looked up to find that she was staring toward the south. "We should find some sort of shelter, and it'll be harder in the dark."

"Right." Viktor nodded and reached up to tuck a strand of hair behind one ear. His fingers left a smudge of purple on his temple. "Do you know this area of town?"

"Not really."

"Léa?"

I shook my head.

"Our place was in C-Roy's territory," Viktor said.

Katja frowned. "Your place?"

"My aunt and uncle's place. Not our place up in Niesha's turf."

She nodded. "I know I said I never wanted to see a Cheeznudle again, but I really miss having a stocked kitchen. Or any kitchen at all." With a sigh, she started to walk. "Come on. Maybe we'll find a park or something. It shouldn't be too dangerous with four of us."

Buddy trotted after her, so of course Click followed. I didn't move. Neither did Viktor.

"Do you trust her?" I asked quietly.

"Do you?"

"I have no reason not to."

He made a non-committal sort of noise. I shoved the rest of the berries into my mouth, then wiped my hands on the sides of my jacket. It was already stained, anyway.

"Feel better after your dessert?" he asked. I turned to him, not quite sure if he was making some sort of joke that my starved brain just wasn't getting. But all I saw on his features was a gentle expression, somewhere between concern and affection. I felt my cheeks rush with heat, and I quickly looked away.

"I guess."

He stepped closer and slipped his arm around my shoulders for a quick squeeze. "You're all right," he said softly, tipping his mouth close to my ear. Before I could even react, though, he'd already pulled away and was walking quickly after the others. "Let's just make sure it's not a dog park," he called out into the deepening evening. "I don't want to sleep on dog poop."

CHAPTER 7

WEIRDOS EVERYWHERE

The nights got pretty cool, so I was glad I still had my jacket. I wore the hood up, partly for warmth and partly to keep bugs out of my hair. I didn't think I'd ever spent so much time sleeping on grass. Even before I'd met Viktor and Click, I had never slept so rough.

I awoke in the morning after a restless sleep to find a heavy hand on my arm. Craning my neck back to look, I spotted Viktor, fast asleep. He wasn't close enough to be sharing any of his body heat, and, for a moment, I felt a twang of regret. But I squelched it down as I sat up slowly, allowing his hand to fall to the grass. He didn't stir.

It was well past dawn, though not so late that it was starting to get warm. Katja sat a few feet away, limbs folded tightly. She had a hoodie, but it wasn't helping her shorts-clad bottom half. I could see the goosebumps on her legs from where I sat.

"Morning," she said quietly. I just nodded. She

glanced at Click, who was curled up on his side next to her, Buddy snuggled against his chest. "How do these guys take to being woken up?"

"Huh?"

"Are they morning people? Or will we get our heads bitten off?"

I looked at Viktor, who still seemed to be fast asleep. "They're fine."

"Good. Because we should get going." She shivered and stood up. "I'm going to the bathroom." She pointed, and I followed her finger over to a gaudily decorated (aka vandalized) building at the edge of the park.

I shuddered. "Go ahead."

"What?"

"Those haven't been cleaned in three years."

She said nothing. Eventually, she just shook her head and started walking over there. I let her go and looked around for another place to relieve myself. I only had to pee, so bushes would do . . . as long as they weren't blackberry bushes. I didn't particularly feel like getting scratched *there*.

"Maybe she's shy," Viktor said. I turned back quickly, only to see that his eyes were still closed.

"Were you eavesdropping?"

"I was sleeping."

"Right."

He opened his good eye and peered at me. "What else would I have been doing?"

"Eavesdropping."

He sighed and rolled onto his back to stare up at the morning sky. "Alas. I missed the juicy girl talk."

I snorted. "All we talked about was dirty bathrooms."

He turned to me, eyebrow quirked.

"Sorry to disappoint you."

"I'll live." He sat up and brushed the grass from his hands. His ponytail was looking a little worse for wear, but he didn't bother to reach up to adjust it. He just rubbed his hands over his cheeks and yawned widely. "What kind of food do you think Rasputin has? Spaghetti? Steak?"

"Maybe they only have raisins."

He pretended to gag.

"Says the guy who thinks nothing of chowing down on a tree."

"Hey! Pine trees are tasty. I think I'm becoming something of a connoisseur." He unzipped his jacket and patted the pockets. Finding what he was looking for, he smiled. "And maybe *they'll* be willing to trade."

I looked at the watch glinting in the light and shook my head. "If Rasputin's anything like the other bosses, they'll probably be too young to care about an antique like that."

"It's not that old," he said, turning it to peer closely at the dial.

"My point still stands."

"We don't know how old Rasputin actually is." He finally pushed the watch back into his pocket and wrapped his arms around his bent knees as he stared at me. "I've only heard rumours."

"Like what?"

He snorted. "Same sort of spit that flies around about everything in this town. Urban legends. Conspiracy theories."

"Who's conspiring?"

"I don't know. But I'm sure the bosses make deals from time to time."

"Did Niesha?"

He shrugged. "Maybe. But if she did, she never told me about—"

"She did," Katja said. I turned to find her hurrying back toward us, looking a little green. "God. You were right, Léa." She shuddered as she sat down. Buddy must've felt it through the grass, because his head immediately popped up. He extricated himself from Click's embrace, wandered over to Katja, and tried to climb into her lap. She arranged her legs to make it easier for him. "Niesha and Ryver had some sort of arrangement."

"Really?" I said, frowning. "I didn't know that."

"Neither did I," Viktor said.

Katja rolled her eyes. "You were hardly upper management. And, anyway, it only happened a couple of times. Last year. During the Shortage."

"Hardly a shortage," Viktor said. "So there was no meat for a couple of months. Big deal."

She looked at him like he was a moron. "Was there meat outside the Zone?"

"Yeah . . . I guess. We only had one meal while we were out there, so—"

"Xavi thought it might've been some sort of experiment. Like, they wanted to see what would happen to our powers if they cut off our protein source."

"We still had protein," Viktor pointed out. "Lots of beans. Lots of farts."

"I'm sure you know all about that."

He grinned, which was all the answer we needed.

"Niesha thought it was more likely something to do with the runners," Katja went on. "It's not hard to divert a supply when you've got control."

"So who had the control? It certainly wasn't us."

"And King Joshua really ramped the raids up at that time, so he was hurting, too. My guess is that Permanent Marc's guys diverted quite a bit of food. From the northern checkpoints, anyway." She shrugged. Her fingers were massaging Buddy's scruffy ears. He seemed to be in a state of bliss. "We'll probably never know. There's probably a lot we'll never know."

"Like what?"

She gave him a funny look. "Like how we ended up stuck in this hellhole?"

"Ah. Well, you see, Katja, there was an incident at the high school, and to protect the general public, Kenyonville was—"

"I know that part, smartass. I'm talking about the Rift itself."

He shrugged. "Aliens?"

"I doubt it."

"Then what's your theory?"

"I don't have one." She moved her fingers under Buddy's chin and gave it a gentle scratch. "Maybe the urban legend is true."

"Which urban legend?" I asked.

"Cody Lamoreaux and the Science Project of Doom."

I let out a grunt of amusement. "The what?"

"You've heard of Cody Lamoreaux, right?"

"Only in passing."

She frowned. "You didn't know him from school?"

"Léa was homeschooled," Viktor said, leaning toward her and lowering his voice to a stage whisper. "If she seems a little weird, that's probably why."

"Shut up," I said, not even bothering to turn to him to deliver the command. "What was the Science Project of Doom?"

"Hell if I know," Katja said. "That's just the story that's been floating around for the last three years. Maybe Cody was just some poor kid who got scapegoated. He hasn't been seen since this all started."

"Maybe he didn't exist in the first place."

"He existed," Viktor said. "I remember seeing him at school."

"Then where is he?"

Katja shook her head slowly. "If you believe the rumours, he either died from a virus that came through the Rift—"

"It's not viral," Viktor interjected.

"Then maybe the radiation from the Rift killed him."

"There were other kids in that science lab. Wouldn't they have died, too?"

"Yeah. I'm just sharing the theories." She lifted Buddy off her lap and brushed the dog hair from her shorts. Buddy shook himself out and stared at her longingly. "My favourite theory, though, is the one where he got hauled off by the men in black."

"For what?" I asked.

"Creating the Rift."

"How?"

She shrugged. "Who knows?"

I frowned. It didn't seem likely that a high school science project could've ripped a hole in spacetime... or whatever the hell the Rift actually was. But I supposed anything was possible. You could find out how to do all sorts of things online. Maybe this Cody guy had been messing around with something that he really should've left alone.

"So, what's the plan?" Viktor asked, drawing my attention back to him. "Do you want to find Rasputin this morning, or do you want to forage first?"

"I don't really want to do either," Katja said. "But if I have to choose one of those, I'd rather find Rasputin. I just want some real food."

"And a real bed," I added, the words slipping out before I could stop them.

Katja nodded. "That, too. I'm hoping they'll have

someplace we can stay. At this point, I'll settle for a worn-out couch."

Viktor let out a groan that sounded almost sexual in nature. Katja turned to him with a frown.

"What's your problem?"

"Stop putting ideas in my head."

"What? Couches?"

He let out another groan and flopped backward onto the grass. Katja turned to me, looking perplexed.

"If you ignore him," I said, "maybe he'll stop."

"Has that worked so far?"

Both of us already knew the answer to that question, so I didn't bother to say anything.

—

Part of Rasputin's territory was a newer area of town. Unlike Main Street with its renovated buildings that had been there for decades, the southwestern quadrant of Kenyonville was relatively new and kind of swanky. There were boutiques whose names suggested fine clothes, fine imported foods, and fine wines . . . although none of them looked like they'd sold anything, fine or otherwise, in years. Still, they looked less like victims of an apocalypse and more like closed businesses in a slightly neglected area of town.

But as we moved farther into the territory, I started to feel more and more uneasy. I couldn't really figure out why. Things didn't *look* too bad. Maybe that was part of it; the relative normalness seemed . . . wrong. I wasn't sure if the others were feeling the same thing, but I would not have been surprised. Everyone was quiet. Even Viktor.

"Does anyone know where we're going?" Katja asked quietly, glancing at Viktor, then at me. When I shook my head, she sighed. "Great."

"We'll just have to ask for directions," Viktor said. He peered down a suspiciously clean alley between two buildings. "So much for dumpster diving."

"Do you really think anyone would throw out anything good?"

"Yeah. You're right. I don't want secondhand raisins."

She glanced at him. "Are you seriously that picky?"

"Do *you* want dumpster raisins?"

"It doesn't matter where they come from if—"

"Guys," I said, shuffling to a quick stop. They both turned and looked at me. Click came to a stop, too, while Buddy wandered a little ahead and sniffed at something in the gutter.

"What?" Viktor asked, whipping his head around to look down the street. "Oh. Spit."

"Isn't that what we were looking for?" Katja asked.

"We're looking for Rasputin. Not some random kid with a . . ." He squinted. "What is that?"

"Blow gun? Staff?"

Viktor snorted. "Pinkhands aren't enough?"

"It's probably for show. Just like King Joshua and his little guns."

"Um, excuse me. Those things sting."

She turned to him with a frown. "They shot at you?"

"Yeah. Almost took out my good eye, too." He turned back to the figure who was crouched about a block away, right in the middle of the sidewalk. "We better not be dealing with the same level of batspittery here."

Katja snorted in amusement, then shook her head. "This whole town has gone batshit, Viktor. Besides, there are four of us and one of them."

"Click doesn't have pinkhands."

"Okay, fine. But my point stands. And if we want to find Rasputin—"

"Maybe that *is* Rasputin."

She made a dismissive noise and strode forward. "How many bosses do you know who act like that?" With a wave of her hand to indicate the weird squatting kid, she looked back over her shoulder. "You coming?"

I didn't really want to, and Viktor didn't seem too crazy about the idea, either. Wandering around in familiar territories was one thing. We knew what to expect: power-hungry teenagers in Niesha's old territory; wannabe tough guys in Joshua's; lazy sunbathers in Ryver's; kids pretending to be adults in C-Roy's; and absolute psychopaths in Permanent Marc's. But Rasputin's turf? I'd never ventured into it on my own in the three years since the Rift. So I had no idea what to expect.

"What do you think?"

I looked up to find Viktor waiting for an answer, his eyebrows raised. Turning, I peered after Katja. Buddy had followed her, so Click was following him. I shook my head. "I don't know."

"We can try talking to Xavi."

I frowned. "We're not welcome there."

"No, Katja's not welcome there."

"So you want to ditch her?"

"I didn't say that."

"You kind of implied it."

He sighed and reached up to tighten his ponytail.

"What's wrong?" I asked.

"Nothing. We're just about to wander into some mysterious boss' territory. We could be walking into . . ."

"What?" I asked. My voice shook a little. Viktor didn't seem to be afraid of much, but something was making him uneasy. He looked at me, a frown creasing his features. But it only lasted for a moment before seeming to dissolve.

"Never mind. I get paranoid when I'm hungry."

"Yeah?"

"Yeah."

"So go eat a tree."

He let out a bark of laughter. "You *really* don't like my cooking, do you?"

"Pulling pine needles off a branch is hardly cooking. Buddy can do that, and he's just a stupid dog."

He blinked his mismatched eyes. "Are you equating my intelligence to Buddy's?"

In response, I just drew my shoulders up to my ears. He laughed again and reached out to put his arm around me, sweeping me forward. I grunted and pushed away from him.

"Gross. You stink."

"Like what?"

"Do you really want me to answer that?"

He pretended to think about the question. I just rolled my eyes.

When we caught up to Katja and Click, they were standing still, just a few feet away from the weird kid, who hadn't moved from their crouch. I wasn't sure if they were male or female. They hadn't had a haircut in years, at any rate. Their brown hair was so matted that it was almost like a solid helmet. I couldn't determine an age, either; they looked young, almost the age of Viktor's cousin. It was certainly possible, if they'd gone through puberty a little earlier than usual. The long object they carried (I could see that it was just a walking stick) was braced against the sidewalk beside a pair of filthy bare feet. The kid was wearing shorts and a t-shirt, both of which looked fairly new and clean. It was a weird contrast with the grubby feet and matted hair.

Okay. Pretty much *everything* about this kid was weird.

"Greetings, Earthling," Viktor said, which drew the kid's attention upward. Their light brown eyes scanned over Viktor's features for a few seconds before seeming to stick on one side of his face. Maybe they felt some sort of affinity with him, since they were sporting an inch-long scar of their own on the left cheekbone. It looked like a burn from Rift energy.

"Hey," the kid said. The voice didn't clear much up. It was youthful and fairly high.

"Nice day."

"Yup."

"Cool place for a squat."

"Uh-huh."

Viktor glanced at me. I shrugged.

"You have a name?" Katja asked. The kid turned their gaze to her; the rest of their body didn't move.

"Yeah, but only my friends get to know it."

"I'm Katja. This is Viktor, Léa, and Click."

"And that's Buddy," Viktor added, pointing at the dog who'd sat down beside Katja's feet. He was staring at the kid, head cocked, like he didn't know what to make of them, either.

"Okay," the kid said.

"So . . . can we be friends?" Katja asked.

The kid stood up, smoothly rising out of their crouch. They were shorter than all of us, and pretty skinny. My heart sank a little. Maybe aligning ourselves with Rasputin wasn't going to be the meal ticket we expected.

"You'll have to agree," they said, then thumped their stick on the ground three times.

"Agree to what?"

"Follow me." They turned and walked down the sidewalk. The rest of us glanced at each other. I could see the unease in Viktor's and Katja's expressions. My face probably looked the same (or worse). But we weren't going to get any answers just standing there, so we started walking, following the barefoot kid with the walking stick.

CHAPTER 8

FOLLOWERS

Everything just seemed to be getting weirder. As we walked, we started to see more people. But they looked just as weird as the kid we were following (bad hair days all around, mismatched ensembles, and bare feet), which seemed even odder given the surroundings. If you didn't know any better, you might've thought that it was just a holiday and all the businesses were simply closed. Hardly any windows were broken, and those that were had been covered with various objects: pieces of plywood, sheets of metal, or blankets. It looked like there was some sort of order . . . which was even stranger, given that most of these kids were younger than us.

"*Lord of the Flies* . . ." Viktor mumbled, staring at a trio of grubby-looking girls who just stood there, watching us walk past.

"That was a bunch of boys," I pointed out.

He shook his head. "I was referring to the leadership. Or lack thereof."

"Rasputin."

"Yeah. For all we know, they might be fifteen years old."

"Or they might be twenty-five," I said, warily watching another group of kids as we passed. They seemed to be appearing out of nowhere.

"Then why can't they get any older Rifters to stick around?"

"Maybe they're just not out roaming the streets."

He frowned. "Upper management probably doesn't want to risk their necks around outsiders."

I snorted. "You're assuming Rasputin has everything structured logically. Maybe there is no upper management. Maybe it's just them at the top, calling the shots."

"Like a cult?"

I nodded. "Look at these kids."

"What about them?"

I edged a little closer to him so I could lower my voice. "Is it just me, or have there been an awful lot of accidents with Rift energy in this part of town?"

"I don't think those are accidents." He came to a sudden stop and looked down at me. "Spit. Think Rasputin was inspired by Permanent Marc?"

My hand drifted to my left cheek, almost automatically. I turned back to Viktor, who was looking at me with a weird expression. "What?" I said.

"It's no big deal for me. But you . . ."

"You think I'm that vain?"

"No. But I think you're pretty, and I don't want you messing up your face. One disfigured person in this group is enough."

My cheeks went hot. I dropped my hand. "It's a small price to pay to avoid starvation," I said. "Besides . . . it's not like I'm ever getting out of here, so it doesn't matter what anyone outside the Rift thinks."

"What about inside the Rift? You think if we get marked by Rasputin, we'll be welcome anywhere else?"

"We're not welcome anywhere else as it is."

He sighed and bit his lip as he tightened his ponytail. "You know it's going to hurt like a bunny, right?"

I nodded, looking up at the ruined side of his face. I'd only ever had minor burns from Rift energy, but enough to know how powerful it was. A tiny little spark of that stuff hurt a lot more—and burned far deeper—than a regular flame. Before I could think too much about it, I reached up and let my fingers trail over his scar. He looked at me, eyebrow quirked.

"Does it still hurt?"

"It's tight. Not painful, though." He shook his head slowly, so I pulled my hand away. "Are you *sure*, Léa? I know you're hungry, but—"

"I'm not hungry. I'm desperate. And I'm the reason we're down here in the first place."

"No, *I'm* the reason we're down here in the first place."

"Huh?"

"I dragged you back into the Zone." He bit his lip again. He wouldn't look at me. "I just . . ."

"I know."

He closed his eyes and shook his head.

"When you find someone who can stand you, you hang on to them. Right?"

A small bark of laughter escaped his lips, and he opened his eyes. "You can actually stand me?"

"Some days." I gave him a little smile. It was hard, given everything swirling around me at that moment. Fear. Uncertainty. Guilt. The ever-present hunger that gnawed so hard that I was afraid I was going to end up with a hole in my stomach.

"I'll take it." He sucked in a deep breath, then let it out slowly. "You're *sure* you want to do this? There aren't any plastic surgeons in town to undo it if you change your mind."

I nodded, even though I wasn't sure at all, and pulled my gaze away from him. Katja, Click, and the grungy kid were about a block away, waiting for us. I grabbed Viktor's hand and pulled him after me, trying to push my worries aside.

I'd lived through losing a toe. I could live with a little scar . . . especially if it came with a meal.

—

"Well," Viktor said as we stood in front of the frosted-glass façade. "This is *not* what I was expecting."

Smile & Shine Cosmetic Dentistry seemed to have fared pretty well. Its glass doors and windows were all intact, and I could even see lights on inside. When the kid who'd been leading us grasped the brushed metal handle on the door, I was struck by how incongruous it looked. They yanked open the door, and I sucked in a breath as the sensation of weirdness only grew.

"Is that air-conditioning?" Katja asked incredulously.

"We had air-conditioning at our place," Viktor said, grabbing the edge of the open door and waving the rest of us inside. I let Katja and Click go first. Buddy trotted in after them, his nails clicking on the smooth stone floor. I glanced up at Viktor as I passed, and he gave me a quick, regretful smile. He was probably still thinking about my face. All I could think about at that moment was my stomach, though.

The reception area looked pristine. The computer that should've been behind the desk was gone, but other than that, the place looked much like any other business before the Rift. The waiting area's benches were intact, clean, and improbably white. Large landscape photos still hung on the walls. There were even stacks of magazines sitting on the tables between the benches. When I peered a little closer, I saw what they were. I nudged Viktor to get him to look. He snorted.

"Someone must've been trading with Joshua."

"You think he'd give those up?"

"If they didn't get the job done anymore, yeah." He looked around the rest of the space, then settled his gaze on the kid who'd led us in, who was standing beside the reception desk, wooden stick at their side.

"Have a seat," they said with an air of professionalism that didn't really match their grubby appearance. "Rasputin will be with you shortly." Then they turned and walked through a doorway at the back of the space, stick tapping on the floor.

"Should we have made an appointment?" Viktor asked. I gave his arm a gentle whack. "What? I'm just asking."

Katja sighed and went to sit down on one of the benches. Buddy followed and jumped up onto the padded surface beside her. She gave him an absent scratch behind the ears as she peered at the nearest magazine.

"Should we get a subscription to that one?" Viktor asked. She didn't dignify that with an answer. Instead, she looked around the space.

"I didn't think there were any places like this left in Kenyonville."

"Your house looked pretty clean when I saw it," I said.

She shook her head and tucked the greenish strand of hair behind her ear. "I'm sure there are plenty of clean houses. I meant businesses. Most of those have been trashed."

I thought of Joshua's throne room in the old phone boutique. "Trashed" wasn't quite adequate.

"This is a good sign," Viktor said, striding over and sitting down beside her. He stretched his long legs out in front of him. "If someone's taking care of the place, then they're feeling up to it. Housekeeping is probably the first thing to go out the window when you're hungry."

"What was your excuse?" I muttered. He turned to me with a quirked eyebrow.

"What was wrong with our house?"

"Oh, I don't know. It smelled like armpit, for one thing."

"Whose armpit? Yours?"

"Shut up."

Katja grunted and shook her head. "Are you two always like this?"

"Actually," Viktor said, leaning closer to her as if he were about to share a secret, "this is Léa when she's being *nice*. Yeah. When she's not, be prepared to have your self-esteem obliterated."

I opened my mouth to retort, but quickly shut it again as memories of all the barbs I'd ever slung at him came rushing back. Folding my arms across my chest, I turned away.

"Click and I are used to it," he went on. "Aren't we?"

Click gave him a thumbs up. I glared at him. He just stared back at me, then smiled brightly.

"I got stuck with you," I said, turning back to Viktor so I could glare at him properly. "I certainly wouldn't have chosen to live in the Basement of Stench willingly."

"None of this was by choice," Katja said. "The Rift took most of our choices away." She picked at a thread on the edge of her shorts. Viktor watched her for a moment, a deep frown creasing his features.

"What choices would you make if you could?"

She turned to him in disbelief. "Are you serious?"

"Sometimes, yeah."

She shook her head. "If I weren't stuck here, I'd be out in the world. Dating. Making a life for myself."

"You can do those things here."

"Maybe *you* can. Would you want to be a lesbian in a town where arousal equals Rift energy coursing through your fingers?"

"How do you know it doesn't course through other things?"

She blinked. "Does it?"

He shrugged and turned to me. "Dunno. Haven't had a chance to test that theory yet."

"Gross," I said. "Don't even think about it."

"Too late."

"Shut up!"

Katja couldn't hide her amusement. She shook her head and concentrated on giving Buddy a good head rub.

"I should probably do some experiments," Viktor said. "You know. For science."

"With your track record," I said, "you'd probably burn your dick off."

He coughed, indignant. "Excuse me?"

"You couldn't even manage shaving without frying half your face. You think you'd be able to jerk off without having a weenie roast?"

Katja burst out laughing and finally abandoned the dog. "Excuse me? Shaving? What the hell were you shaving?" She grabbed his chin in her hand and turned it left and right.

"A guy can dream, can't he?"

"Dreams can only take you so far."

"Fair enough." He pulled out of her grasp and leaned back against the window. "I don't know if you're aware, but I'm really good at controlling pinkhands."

"Looks like it."

"I'm not talking about back then. I barely knew what I was dealing with when this happened." He waved his hand, indicating the side of his face. "But now . . . How do you think we got out of here last month?"

She blinked. "I thought you snuck out."

"Nope. We walked right up to the checkpoint and asked to leave."

"And they *let* you?"

"After we convinced them we didn't have pinkhands anymore."

"But you do."

"Well, *we* know that. But there was no reason for *them* to know that."

She shook her head slowly. "So how did you . . ."

"We grounded it," I said, drawing her attention toward me.

"Grounded it?"

"Yeah," Viktor said. "You just drive it down into the ground through your feet. It's easy. Even Léa could do it."

"Not very well," I muttered.

"I had your back, didn't I?"

I shrugged and looked away.

"So I could *totally* do the horizontal hula without frying anything. I'm that good."

Katja grunted. "You are, are you?"

"So I've been told."

"Oh, my god, Viktor," I said, causing him to turn toward me in surprise. "You're seventeen fucking years old and you've been stuck in here for the last three years. Unless you were screwing girls as a freshman—"

"I don't *screw*," he said. "I make love. Gently."

Katja and I looked at each other. And then we both burst into peals of laughter. Viktor grinned and leaned his head back against the glass, seemingly satisfied. I didn't believe him, and Katja probably didn't, either.

But it felt good to laugh.

CHAPTER 9

PRELUDE TO ODONTOPHOBIA

I had no idea what was taking so long.

Maybe making us wait was some sort of psychological game. There were no sounds coming from the back of the business. None that I could hear, anyway. It was hard to hear much over the growling of my stomach.

"You're *really* hungry, aren't you?" Viktor observed.

"Shut up. So are you."

"At least I'm quiet about it."

"Oh, I'm sorry. I forgot you had control over your growling stomach. You're so *talented*."

He shook his head and closed his eyes, still leaning back against the window. "Maybe someone had an appointment before us."

I opened my mouth to retort, then closed it again. It was possible. There wasn't that much switching of alliances after three years . . . but it did happen. We were proof of that.

"Maybe they're on their lunch break," he added.

"Unless they're willing to share, I don't want to hear about it." I stalked to the door and tried to peer out through the lettering, which was the only part that wasn't frosted. The sun was high in the sky. It was probably close to noon. Lunchtime. It was strange how, even after so many months of sporadic food, I still thought in terms of regular meals.

"If they're not willing to share, we're out of here," Katja said. "That was the whole point. We can starve to death anywhere. And I'd prefer to do it somewhere without a bunch of feral children watching."

"We're not feral," a voice said. I spun around, only to see the kid from earlier, walking stick still in hand. "Rasputin will see you now."

"Oh." The word dropped out of my mouth and hung in the space. None of us moved. I looked over at Viktor, then at Katja, and finally at Click. They just returned my gaze with something I couldn't really read. It took a moment to realize they were waiting for me to say something. I swallowed hard, realizing how dry my mouth was. "Let's go?"

Katja stood up and headed for the back of the room. Buddy and Click followed. But Viktor moved more slowly. He unfolded himself from the bench and stood, his gaze fixed on me.

"You sure?" he mouthed. I nodded before I could really think about it. He nodded back, then reached out and took my hand. I let him, even though my hand was sweaty and I felt like I was on the verge of erupting into a bad case of pinkhands. Taking a deep breath, I tried to ground the energy, pushing it down toward my feet and imagining it seeping into the ground with each step.

Through the doorway at the back of the space was a short hall, clean and somewhat dimly lit with ornamental sconces. The grungy kid stood beside a doorway about halfway down, free hand stretched to one side to usher us into the room. We filed in slowly. I sucked in a breath.

It looked like something out of a reality TV show, the kind that followed rich people doing rich-people stuff. Soft instrumental music played on invisible speakers. A diffuser misted on a corner table, filling the space with a sweet, earthy scent that reminded me of spring and dew. Sleek white cupboards lined the walls. In the middle of the space sat a white chair that sort of looked like the kind in my old dentist's office. This one looked a hell of a lot nicer, though.

Behind the chair, side by side, stood two young adults. Brother and sister, from the look of it. Twins, if I had to guess. They both had the same straight, dark hair and pale blue eyes. They were also a lot cleaner than the kid with the walking stick. In fact, they looked like they'd probably showered that morning and put on clean clothes. Their feet were bare but pristine. As the four of us crowded into the room, the twins turned to look at each other. They gave a quick nod, then turned their attention back to us.

"Welcome," they said, their voices so in unison that it seemed to cause some sort of resonant effect. I shuddered.

"Thanks," Viktor said. "We're looking to relocate, and we thought your territory looked nice."

The girl smiled, but the expression didn't go all the way to her eyes. She regarded Viktor for a few seconds, taking in his appearance. He squeezed my hand. It almost felt like he was trembling.

"You're looking for work?" the boy asked. His gaze was drawn to the floor. I looked and saw Buddy cowering against Click's leg. For a moment, a surge of panic flared through me. I quickly diverted the energy down through my legs so I didn't burn Viktor's hand. *This place probably just reminds him of the vet's office*, I told myself. *Lots of white. Too clean. Air-conditioning. That's all it is.*

"If you've got some," Katja said. "But we're hammering out the terms first. I don't want you pulling some stunt where you get us to risk our necks and then don't pay us."

All four of the twins' eyebrows rose.

"And I want to make the deal with Rasputin," Katja went on. "Not their lackeys."

The girl laughed. "Who do you think you're talking to?"

Katja frowned.

"You're Rasputin?" I asked. The girl turned to me with a smirk.

"Surprised?"

"You realize nobody in the rest of Kenyonville knows anything about you," Viktor said. "Everyone assumes you're a single person with they-them pronouns."

"Maybe that's how we like it." Her gaze fixed itself on the side of his face. "What happened there?"

"Rift bear tried to chew my head off."

Her eyes narrowed.

"Do you have any work or not?" Katja asked. "If not, we don't need to waste any more time here."

"There's always work," the boy said. "If you're willing."

"Why wouldn't we be willing to work?"

He shook his head. "That's not what I meant."

"Then what . . . ?" She trailed off and looked over at the open door. The grungy kid was still there, like they were standing guard. "Fuck. Are you serious?"

The twins said nothing.

Katja turned to us. "You realize there's a dress code here, right?"

"The scar?" Viktor asked. "Yeah. We know." His voice was flat.

"Shit, Viktor! Why didn't you say anything?"

"I thought you knew."

She shook her head. "Not happening. I'm not *that* hungry."

My brain—and stomach—started to panic. My throat felt like it was stuffed with a sock. I needed to cry . . . but I still couldn't. "So leave," I managed to choke out.

She stared at me like I'd lost my mind. "Are you serious?" She looked up at Viktor, then shook her head. "You're both batshit. If I wanted to fuck up my face, I would've just gone to Permanent Marc."

"I don't think *his* face can get much worse," the boy said, jerking his chin at Viktor. Katja turned to glare at him.

"Well, mine can. So you can suck it." She looked at me and Viktor. I averted my gaze. Viktor squeezed my hand even more tightly. "Unbelievable." She shook her head and stormed to the doorway. "Out of my way," she growled, pushing her way past the kid with the stick. They let her go.

"Bah-dee!" Click called, his voice desperate. I looked down to see a flash of white as the little dog pursued Katja out the door. Click followed, of course. I turned to Viktor, whose jaw was twitching.

"Thought you guys wanted work," the girl said.

Viktor nodded. "We do."

"No mark, no job."

"It's fine. He'll be back once he finds his dog."

"We're ready," I added. But I wasn't sure I was. My heart was slamming around so hard in my chest that it felt like my whole body was shaking. Viktor must've been able to feel it. "First, though, tell us about the job."

"Runner," the girl said. She tapped her own cheekbone, which was smooth. "This is how the guys at the checkpoint know who to give the food to."

I frowned. "But everyone here has—"

"They like to feel like they belong." She tapped her cheekbone again, and I noticed she was tapping the right side . . . not the left. "Right: runner. Left: lackey."

Viktor snorted. "You call them lackeys?"

"What else would we call them? That's what they are, aren't they?"

I looked up at Viktor and gave his hand a squeeze. He turned to look down at me.

"What?" he asked.

"You really want to mess up the good side of your face?"

"If you can do it, why can't I?"

I shook my head. "It's not—"

"You're hungry. Let's just do this and get it over with." He turned back to Rasputin, who were just standing there watching us. Now that I thought about it, I didn't think they'd moved the whole time. "How do you want to do this?"

The girl gestured to the chair. Viktor started to step forward, but I tugged on his hand, bringing him to a stop.

"No. I'll go first."

"Why?"

"Because . . ." Shaking my head, I pulled my hand out of his. "Just because." I stepped forward and climbed onto the cool chair. The fake white leather squeaked a little under me as I got myself settled. Viktor stood off to the side, a deep frown creasing his features. A movement drew my attention to my left, and I turned to see the boy take something blue out of one of the cupboards. He stepped closer, and I heard the unmistakeable ripping sound of hook-and-loop fabric.

"What is that?" Viktor asked, his voice tense.

"Technically? They're blood pressure cuffs." The boy handed one of the items to his sister before crouching down on my left beside the chair. "Put your arms on the armrests."

My hands shook as I did so. The boy wrapped the blue cuff around my forearm and the armrest—tightly—making sure the hook-and-loop closure was secure. His sister followed a similar procedure on my right. As I looked over at Viktor, I could feel my eyes getting wider and wider. He gave his head a little shake and took a step forward.

"It's for your own protection," the boy said, and I turned to look at him. His eyes looked even paler up close.

"Why?"

"Because you're going to struggle once the Rift fire hits your skin," the girl said. "Everyone does." She stood up, giving my wrist a pat. I curled my hands into fists and strained against the cuffs, testing their strength. There was barely any movement, and a surge of panic swept through me.

"Do you have a job for us?" I asked, which seemed to take both of them aback. I took a deep breath. "When we're done. Do you have a job we can do?"

"Not today," the boy said.

"But—"

"Tomorrow. And we'll give you some food today. That's what you really want, right?"

I made a little noise that might've been an acknowledgement, but it sounded more like a squeak. The girl smiled and reached forward to tuck my hair back behind my ears. Her eyes were just as pale as her brother's . . . but with a further coolness that I found unnerving. She nodded to the boy, and he went to stand behind me. I looked desperately at Viktor, just as a pair of hands grabbed my head and pulled it back against the headrest.

"You'll want to sit still for this," the girl said. "It looks better when it's a nice, clean thumbprint."

I screwed my eyes shut. The boy's fingers felt hot against my head. I braced every part of my body I could think of. I even curled my nine toes inside my shoes.

"Léa—" Viktor began.

"It's okay. Just . . . wait your turn."

He didn't say anything. But I could hear everything now. The boy breathing behind me. The girl breathing beside me. The squeak of my butt on the fake leather. The sound of my overgrown toenails scraping the toe boxes of my sneakers. I took a deep breath and held it.

The pain was almost visible as the girl pressed her thumb against my cheek. I knew I wasn't just seeing the pink Rift energy through my eyelids, either, because what I saw was yellow . . . then white . . . then blue. I sucked in a gasp and tried to draw my hands toward me. But, of course, I couldn't move. I felt—and heard—the girl pull her thumb away, but the pain continued, making my eyes water.

"Breathe," Viktor's voice said, cutting through the fog. The boy finally let go of my head. I drew my knees up and tried to lean forward over them. "Léa, breathe."

I shook my head slowly, which caused my hair to brush against my cheek, and I almost screamed. I sucked in a breath and lifted my head. As I opened my eyes, my vision swam. Viktor stood in front of me, biting his lip.

"You're all right," he said softly.

But you're not, I thought. One small, thumbprint-sized burn was almost more than I could bear. When I thought about him three years earlier, imagining that pain multiplied by at least ten . . . And I was asking him to go through it again.

"Take these off," I said, looking down at my hands. I pulled hard, but the restraints were too tight. "Take them off!" My voice rose to a shout. The boy ripped off the left cuff, then the right. I was out of that chair before he could even step away, barrelling into Viktor, who caught me and held me as I stood there, shaking, my forehead pressed against his chest. "I changed my mind."

"What?"

"I changed my mind," I whimpered. "I'll eat a tree. Just . . . Let's go."

He pulled back and leaned down so he could look me in the eye. His gaze drifted to my cheek, and he brushed his thumb just below the burn, being so careful. "But you did it."

I focused on his dark eye, trying to stop the tremble in my chin. "I don't want you to have to go through that again."

"And I'm not going to let you go through that for nothing." He straightened up and edged around me, striding to the chair. I turned and watched him, mouth agape.

"Viktor—"

"You think I can't handle it?" He pointed to the ruined side of his face as he sprawled on the chair, crossing his legs casually as if he were getting ready for a routine teeth cleaning. "I mean . . . I'm kind of an expert already."

"What really happened?" the girl asked. Her voice was flat, like she wasn't even interested in the answer. Viktor's eyebrows twitched into a frown as he watched her secure the cuff around his right wrist.

"When?"

"When you got that scar."

"I prefer to think of it as body art."

The boy smirked and tightened the cuff on Viktor's left. He exchanged a look with the girl. She turned back to Viktor.

"Whoever did it did a shitty job."

"Really? I mean, I was going for the supervillain look, so . . . it's pretty spot-on, isn't it?"

"How'd it happen?"

"Rift bear."

"There's no such thing, smartass."

"How do you know? Were you in the science lab when it happened?"

She jerked a little. And then a cold smile spread across her features. Viktor's smile wavered for a moment, but he took a deep breath and blew it out slowly.

"Can we get this done? If Léa doesn't get something to eat soon, she's going to get hangry again. And believe me, you do *not* want to see that."

"Awfully eager to have another scar, aren't you?"

He shrugged as much as he could with his arms pinned to the armrests. "Guess so. If it helps my friends."

"Sit back," the boy said. Viktor did, settling his head against the chair. His feet wiggled nervously back and forth, and I saw him dig his nails into the armrest. My eyes were still watering from the pain, which seemed to be burrowing straight into the bone. I wanted to touch the wound, to see how deep it actually was . . . but I didn't dare.

The girl glanced at me, then exchanged a look with her brother. They both nodded as one.

"Hold him," she said.

Something about the command felt like a block of ice dropped straight into my stomach. My hands flared as my body surged into panic mode, even before I saw the boy grab Viktor's face and peel the eyelids of his good eye back, even before I saw the girl press her thumb against his eyeball.

Even before he started to scream.

CHAPTER 10

THE WORST BEAUTIFUL DAY

"No!" My own scream curled through the air, and I threw myself forward, only to choke as someone grabbed my jacket and yanked so hard that I fell back against the wall, hitting my head. The world sparkled for a moment, and I struggled to see the horrific scene in front of me. Viktor's legs were flailing and his hands were flaring bright pink. And, still, the girl had her thumb pressed against his eye. "Stop! *Stop!*"

To my surprise, she did, pulling back and shaking the Rift energy from her fingers.

"What the fuck is wrong with you?" I screamed.

"What the fuck is wrong with *you?*" she repeated, whirling to face me. Her eyes looked even colder. Like ice. "Do you know who this is?"

"Viktor. Viktor Knowles." My voice was small.

"Viktor Knowles? Is that what he told you?" She

turned back to Viktor, who was still writhing in the chair, almost as if she'd burned him in unmentionable places. "Is that what you told her? Are you fucking serious?"

"I don't . . . I don't understand." I pushed myself to my feet, my legs shaking. My hands were still flaring. I quickly shook them out. The grungy kid, who was standing just inside the doorway, edged away from the splashes. "Viktor, tell her who—"

"His name isn't Viktor."

"Yes, it is."

She turned back to him as he continued to writhe. "You want to tell her, or should I?"

He let out a sob. His eyes were screwed shut, but I could see the tears running down both cheeks.

"Hey, asshole! I said, do you want to tell her, or should I?"

Viktor didn't respond. His hands were still bright pink. The girl regarded him for a moment, then smacked him across the face. Then she spit on him.

"Stop it!" I shouted. "What the hell?"

"This is Cody-fucking-Lamoreaux," she said, her voice low and dangerous. As she spoke, her eyes almost began to glow. "This is the reason we're in this fucking hellhole. This is the reason we've all lost so much. Because some little shit had to go and show off by ripping the Rift through the science lab."

My eyes were wide. Her words bounced around in my head. They didn't make sense. None of this made sense. "You're wrong," I whispered.

"No, I'm not wrong. This asshole destroyed our lives, and then he has the nerve to come here and ask us to *help* him?"

I shook my head. "Viktor, tell them. Tell them who you are!"

"You want more lies? That's all he's given you. He's been hiding here in plain sight. All this time. While people *died* because of what he did."

"He didn't kill anyone."

"Maybe not directly. But every life lost in this fucking nightmare is on him." She turned and looked at him. And then she made a fist and brought it down into his crotch. He squeaked and curled his legs toward his body.

"Whoa," the boy said. "Low blow."

"I don't fucking care! Why are you defending him?" She glared at her brother. "We lost Mom, and thanks to this fucker, we didn't even get to say goodbye."

"What?" I whispered.

"Mom only had weeks to live," she said, turning back to me. "She was in hospice over in Hurstleigh. Then the Rift opened up, and we were *stuck* here." Her eyes narrowed. "So who did *you* lose because of him? Everybody lost someone."

I shook my head. "Viktor, tell them."

"If he denies who he is, he's a liar." She turned back to him. "Did you think we wouldn't recognize you? How fucking stupid do you think we are, Cody?"

I stepped toward the chair. The girl backed up a

little, and I didn't realize why until I looked down and saw the pink. I clenched my fists and drove the energy into my feet. My whole body was buzzing. I didn't know what was Rift energy and what was just adrenaline. "Viktor. You have to tell them."

He pressed his lips together and shook his head.

"Tell them the truth!" I shouted.

"You don't want to hear the truth," the girl said. "Why do you think he hasn't denied it?"

"Because he's in pain! You just—" I broke off as the words caught in my throat. *You just blinded him.* A wave of nausea swept over me. Stepping forward, I reached out and took his face in my hands. He reacted as if I'd burned him, arching his back and letting out a scream. His hands flared anew, and I edged back from the heat I could feel through my clothes.

"Let me go," he rasped. "Let me go!"

I reached for the restraints, but I could see the way he was straining at them, and the way his eyelids were still squeezed so tightly shut, and I knew his first instinct was going to be to press his hand over his wounded eye. "You have to calm down first."

"Fuck that!" he screamed. I didn't know if it was the volume or the word itself that shocked me the most. But it froze me in place, and all I could do was stand there, staring, as he let out god-awful little whimpers that made me want to rip my own ears off. My own cheek was still throbbing, but it seemed like nothing in comparison. The pain that I was imagining was far worse than the reality of what was going on with my own face.

After a few seconds, though, I saw the pink begin to fade. I waited until it was gone before I reached out and ripped the restraints open. The whole time, Rasputin just stood there, two statues. The girl, having spent her venom, was just as quiet as her brother.

"Come on," I whispered, grabbing Viktor's arm and helping him sit up. He slid his legs off the side of the chair and planted his boots on the floor, still keeping his eyes tightly shut. I wasn't even sure if he *could* open them. I remembered getting some medicated shampoo in my eye once; it had stung so bad that my eyes had involuntarily closed and stayed that way for a few minutes until I could rinse them enough to get the suds out. But I knew there was no amount of water that was going to fix what had just been done to Viktor's eye. "Stand up," I said, tugging his arm upward. He did, swaying a little on his feet. "Hold my arm. We're going to walk forward, okay?"

He didn't respond. He just took a step with me. I aimed us toward the door, where the kid with the stick was still standing. They backed up to give us room to pass. I didn't even have the energy to glare at them as we walked into the hall.

The reception area was empty. There was no sign of Katja, Click, or Buddy. But that was the least of my worries. Through the frosted glass, I could see a number of shadows, as if from small figures trying to peer inside. I looked up at Viktor. The unscarred right side of his face was turned toward me, and I could see something trickling down his cheek. It didn't look like tears.

I pushed open the door and led him through, stumbling into the sunlight. The kids who had been trying to see inside scattered like cockroaches. Viktor tensed, as if he could feel the frantic energy of their departure. But he kept walking, unsteadily, letting me lead him out into the midday sun.

What do we do? What am I supposed to do with him? I'm not a doctor. I can't— I sucked in a breath, and immediately my mind tried to create a map of Kenyonville. I wasn't familiar with this area of town. But I knew where we had to go to find someone who could help. We just had to get there.

Viktor's legs seemed heavy, and his toes kept catching every few steps. The sidewalk was too uneven, so I pulled him out into the middle of the street where things were a bit more level. It wasn't like any vehicles were going to come along and hit us. I grabbed his arm with my free hand, but I knew it wasn't going to do much good if he lost his balance. And, sure enough, one painfully slow block later, he tripped and fell. He jerked himself away from me as he did, landing hard on his hands and knees. I bent down to help him back up. But before I could, he lay down, rolling onto his back.

"Viktor, get up."

He pressed his hands against the gritty asphalt. His breaths were quick and pained. It almost seemed like he was trying not to cry.

"Viktor—"

I startled as the roar burst out of him. No, not a roar. A scream. A cacophony. A wretched wail of grief and pain that shook me to my knees. I grabbed the shoulder of his jacket, desperate to get him to stop. But the sound went on for so long. Too long. And, when it was over, he was silent.

"I'm sorry," I whispered. I lay down beside him, staring up at the perversely beautiful sky. He rolled onto his side, away from me, and curled up in the fetal position. I glanced at his back, then turned my gaze to the endless blue, feeling like I needed to really *see* it.

Because he never would again.

———

My brain seemed to have shut off. As we lay in the middle of the street, the sounds of Kenyonville buzzed around us. I heard voices. Birds. The sound of a distant airplane that I couldn't see. But I didn't have any thoughts about any of those things. I didn't have any thoughts at all.

The asphalt was uncomfortably warm. After a while, I sat up and pulled off my jacket. Viktor hadn't made a sound. He was still curled up, but now his palms were pressed over both eyes. Carefully, I reached over and laid my hand on his shoulder. He flinched.

"It's going to be okay." I held my breath, not sure what to expect. If our roles had been reversed and someone had said the same thing to me, I probably would've torn into them. But I didn't know what else to say. He didn't utter a word, though, which was even worse. "We need to get to Dr. Bryan. He might be able to . . ." I bit my lip. I suspected there was only one thing Dr. Bryan was going to be able to do, and I didn't even want to think about it. "Viktor," I whispered, leaning closer so I could smooth back a few loose strands of dark hair. He let out a sob. The sound nearly broke me.

I pulled back and looked around. There was still no sign of the others. Now that we'd been separated, I was really regretting not organizing some sort of rendezvous point for this type of situation. I had no idea where Katja would've gone. Buddy had probably followed her, which meant that Click had followed him. They might've still been together . . . or Click might have been on his way back to us at that moment. I didn't want to make it harder for him to find us. But I also needed to get help for Viktor.

I hauled myself to my feet, grabbed my jacket, and tied the sleeves around my waist. Then I stepped around Viktor and crouched down in front of him.

"Come on," I said, trying to keep my voice gentle. "Get up. I'll help you."

His hands curled into fists. But he still kept them tightly pressed against his eyes.

"You can't stay here for the rest of your life. Let's go see Dr. Bryan. At the very least, he might have something for the pain."

He slowly lowered his hands. But he kept his eyes shut. Up close, I could see that his eyelid looked okay. That was something, at least.

"After we see Dr. Bryan, we'll find Click and Buddy. And then . . . we'll head back to Niesha's territory. Xavi and Crystal might be petty, but they're not monsters. They won't—" I stopped talking as he reached out, groping for my hand. I let him take it. "I won't leave you, okay? I promise."

His chin trembled as he lay there for a moment, squeezing my hand. At last, though, he let go and sat up. Using me to brace himself, he managed to get to his feet. And we started to walk, slowly, back toward Main Street.

—

The lights were off in the vet's office. I didn't say anything to Viktor, but my mind started to freak out. *What day is it? Does he not keep the clinic open on weekends? Viktor needs help now, not in a couple of days.*

"Stay here," I said, moving his hand from my elbow to the post of a no-parking sign. He didn't protest, so I stepped over to the door and tried the handle. As I expected, the door was locked. Cupping my hands around my eyes, I leaned forward and tried to see inside. But there wasn't much I could see, especially with the lights off. I turned away, biting my lip, as I tried to think of an alternate plan. I had no idea where Dr. Bryan actually lived. Ryver might have known . . . but asking would require a trip to the complex and a climb over the wall. Viktor was already looking like he was about to collapse; I doubted he would be up to the trek. And I couldn't leave him while I went by myself. I'd already promised to stay with him.

"Damn it," I said, the words sneaking out before I could stop them. I glanced at Viktor's face, but he didn't seem to have heard me. If he had—if he knew what was going on—he wasn't reacting. I turned back to the door and knocked on the glass. Hard. It was the only thing I could think of. "Dr. Bryan!"

I willed those lights to come on, but the clinic remained dark. Slamming both hands against the glass, I let out a roar of frustration and turned to Viktor, just as he tilted his head back as if he were looking up. The scraping sound registered a moment later. I moved away from the door and looked up at the second storey, shielding my eyes from the sun that was almost in my line of sight.

"Léa?" A familiar face peered down at me through the open window, and a rush of relief almost brought me to my knees. "Are you all right?"

"Viktor needs your help."

He nodded. "I'll be right down." He pulled his head back inside, disappearing from view. I turned to Viktor, who was gripping the pole with so much force that his knuckles were a yellowish white.

"He's coming, okay? Just hold on." I laid my hand on his. He fumbled for it, grasping it tightly. "There's a curb in front of you. Take a step up." I held his hand as he did so, hesitantly, planting his boot on the sidewalk before taking the step. When he was safely over the tricky curb, I led him to the door.

The lights came on inside, and a few seconds after that, Dr. Bryan was at the door. He looked even more casual than the last time I'd seen him, in a t-shirt, khaki shorts, and flip-flops. He almost looked like he was getting ready to take a stroll around a cruise ship deck. He certainly didn't look like someone trapped in the post-apocalyptic Rift Zone. Holding open the door, he waved his hand, ushering us inside. As I led Viktor past him, I could see his gaze focus on Viktor's face. He probably already had an idea of what was wrong.

"Bring him into the exam room," he said. "The light's better." He led us there, even though I already knew the way. I helped Viktor over to the table. Dr. Bryan was grabbing a pair of sterile gloves and pulling them on. "Probably best if you lie down, Viktor. I'll be able to see better."

The table wasn't long enough to accommodate his tall frame, so he had to lie down with his lower legs dangling off the end. But that seemed to be good enough for Dr. Bryan. He approached the table, his expression grim.

"What happened?"

"Some bitch burned his eye," I said, the words coming out sharp, along with a few flecks of spit that I was surprised didn't sizzle and burn where they landed. Dr. Bryan frowned.

"Which eye?"

"The right."

He nodded and stepped around the table to the appropriate side. "Okay, Viktor, I need to have a look. So I want you to try to relax as much as possible, all right? I'll make it quick."

Viktor didn't respond. His hands, though, reached for the edges of the table and gripped them hard. I moved around to the other side, opposite the vet, and peeled the desperate fingers from the table. Then I held his hand in both of mine, pressing it against my chest.

I only caught a glimpse of what was under the eyelid before I had to turn away. Somehow, I managed not to gag or make any sort of noise. Dr. Bryan pulled back a few seconds later and headed to the cupboards at the back of the room. My heart surged as he pulled out a vial and a paper-wrapped syringe.

"What . . ." I began, then shook my head. "How bad is it?"

He said nothing as he brought the supplies back to the table and filled the syringe.

"What is that?"

"A local anesthetic. And I've got some sedation in the other room under lock and key. It's the best I can do." He recapped the now-full syringe and set it aside on a small wheeled cart.

"For what?" I asked. My voice was little more than a whisper. He shook his head and took a deep breath.

"I think you already know. I'm sorry." He placed his hand on Viktor's shoulder. "The burn is too deep. The cornea's been destroyed. It looks like the iris is gone, too."

"But . . ." My tongue seemed to stick in my mouth. "It'll heal, right? Like his other eye? It'll scar, but—"

"No, Léa. If I leave it like this, the dead tissue will eventually cause blood poisoning. It would be medical neglect if I let that happen."

I shook my head. "There has to be something else you can do. Can't you remove just the dead tissue? Or . . ." I trailed off as I saw him shake his head slowly. Turning to Viktor, I regarded his face. His eyes were still screwed tightly shut, so I couldn't really determine his expression. I couldn't tell what he was thinking. His lack of reaction to anything was really starting to scare me. "Viktor, he wants to remove your eye."

His lips pressed together, but he didn't say anything. I looked up at Dr. Bryan, who was watching with a concerned expression.

"He's in a lot of pain," he said quietly. "I know it

probably doesn't sound like it, but the surgery will help."

I shook my head. "I don't want you doing what you did to Floyd."

He looked aghast. "Oh, gosh, Léa. No. We don't do that procedure on humans. I'll spare the eyelid and tear ducts. He can wear an artificial eye if—"

Viktor sat up suddenly, startling both of us. He tried to pull his hand away from me while simultaneously sliding off the end of the table. But Dr. Bryan caught his shoulders.

"Viktor, I know this wasn't the news you wanted to hear. But I can't in good conscience let you walk out of here in this state." He placed one hand under Viktor's chin and tilted his head up a little, as if trying to get a good look at his eye from a different angle. "I'll do the surgery as quickly as I can, all right? Léa can stay here if you want."

My eyes widened. The last thing I wanted to do was watch what was about to happen. But Viktor pulled out of Dr. Bryan's grasp and shook his head. He stood there, breathing hard through his nose, almost as if he were holding back a tidal wave of sobs.

"Can I do the surgery, Viktor?"

The room was quiet. Viktor didn't move for a long time. I knew he was thinking, and his mind was probably racing, trying to work through all the what-ifs. That's what *my* mind was doing, and, as it did, the horrible feeling of regret only grew.

What if I had pulled him out of that dentist's office before he'd sat in that chair?

What if we'd never gone looking for Rasputin?

What if I'd never followed him back into the Rift Zone?

What if I hadn't joined up with him, Click, and Niesha?

What if I had simply done that job for Joshua the way I'd been contracted to do?

Every choice I'd made in the last few months seemed to have led us to our current situation. My choices—my stupid, misguided choices—had led to this. Viktor was blind, and he was going to lose an eye . . . and all because I'd been hungry.

Because I'd been fucking *hungry*.

A wave of anger surged through me, and I felt my hands flare. Dr. Bryan jerked a little in surprise as he noticed the pink.

"Léa? Are you all right?"

But I didn't have a chance to answer him. Viktor let out a long, defeated breath and lay back on the table once more.

"Can I do the surgery?" Dr. Bryan asked again. This time, Viktor gave a little nod. "Okay. Take off your jacket, and I'll administer the sedative." He stepped toward the locked door and fished a set of keys out of his pocket. "Do you want Léa to stay?"

As soon as I saw his head move back and forth on the table, I ran for the waiting room. Shame and relief competed for space as I shook my hands wildly, trying to get rid of the Rift energy. Throwing myself onto one of the chairs, I pulled my legs up to my chest and wrapped my arms around them, making myself as small as possible. But then I thought better of it. I pressed my hands over my ears instead, just in case I heard something that would traumatize me for life.

CHAPTER 11

THINGS WE CAN'T UNSEE

My own heartbeat ticked like a clock in my ears. I could barely breathe, crushed as I was with my forehead resting on my knees. I rocked a little, in time with my heart, trying to think ahead . . . even though the thoughts were so stressful that I wanted to cry.

Finding food had been hard enough before. But now . . . Viktor couldn't even walk without someone to guide him. I didn't even want to think about what this meant for his safety. Using pinkhands would be a shot in the dark. Dodging Riftballs would be next to impossible. So we needed to find someplace safe. A place where we didn't have to worry about being accosted or snuck up on. Of all the territories I'd been in, Niesha's old one probably fit that criteria the best. But there was the small issue of me not being welcome there. And I couldn't just dump Viktor on Xavi and Crystal. Not after I'd promised.

Maybe breaking a promise would end up being the kindest thing, though.

I let out a soft moan as I continued to rock. Weariness crept over me, and all I wanted to do was sleep . . . even though it felt like my whole body was buzzing with adrenaline. My nap of the previous day had been refreshing, but I felt like I needed another one. Lifting my head, I turned to look at the chairs next to me, contemplating their comfort level for a quick nap, and caught sight of movement at the back of the reception area. Dr. Bryan gave me a little smile and walked closer, his flip-flops making their characteristic sound. As he sat down on the chair beside me, I averted my gaze from his t-shirt where I could see a few tiny flecks of blood.

"Is it over?" I asked.

He nodded. "It's done. He'll be out of it for a little while yet. When he's a little more conscious, I want to get him upstairs so he has someplace more comfortable to recuperate."

I swallowed. It felt like there was a peach pit in my throat.

"I had a look at his other eye while he was under," he began, and I sucked in a gasp.

"You didn't—"

He held up his hands. "I didn't touch it. I just wanted to see what was going on there."

"And?"

"He's got pretty severe corneal scarring. But the rest of his eye seems to be okay."

"He can see colour and light," I said.

"That's promising."

"How?" I asked. "Unless you can fix it, he's screwed."

He shook his head. "I can't fix it. But I'm fairly certain it can be fixed with a corneal transplant."

"Right. Because those happen all the time in the Rift Zone." My voice sounded so bitchy. I was too emotionally wasted to care.

"You have to get him out, Léa."

I blinked and turned to him, weirded out by the sudden dark urgency in his voice. He stared back intently, making steady eye contact. "Get him out?" I repeated.

"I don't like what I saw here today. And I'm not talking about his eye. When you were here before, he was . . ."

"Viktor," I said quietly.

"Exactly. This could break him, and if that happens, he's not going to have the support he needs. Not in Kenyonville." He put his hand on my shoulder. "I know you're going to try your best. But he needs more than your friendship can give him. Proper medications, for one thing. Surgery. Fitting an artificial eye. Counselling to deal with what happened."

I nodded and looked down at my knees, which were almost too close to focus on. "I know. But . . . I don't think I can get him out again. Not now. We'd have to cross through Permanent Marc's territory, and even if we made it, if the guards at the checkpoint don't want to help—"

"I'm not talking about a checkpoint."

I sucked in a breath, but I didn't turn to look at him. I just waited for him to go on.

"I have agreements with a certain boss."

I ran through the options in my head, trying to think of the most likely one. "C-Roy?"

"C-Roy?" He sounded puzzled. "Oh. Croydon Masterson. Yes. We've worked out a mutually beneficial arrangement."

"You don't live in his territory."

"I couldn't make a deal with Miss Wells."

I finally turned to look at him. "What kind of arrangement do you have with C-Roy?"

"Quid pro quo. He makes sure some necessary supplies end up in my possession. In return, I provide medical assistance when required."

"Like when my toe got crushed?"

He nodded. "How is it, by the way? Any pain?"

"Not really. Itching, sometimes. That's worse."

"Not much we can do about phantom sensations, I'm afraid."

"I can live with it."

"You can. But I'm not so sure about Viktor." He sighed and looked over at the empty reception desk. "The Zone is dangerous. I don't have to tell you that."

I nodded and looked down at my knees again.

"Croydon has a way out."

I turned to him, my eyes wide. "Then why the hell are you still here?"

He gave me a bemused smile. "You think I should abandon you kids?"

"Everyone else did. Even the aid orgs—"

"I know. And if I'd known that was going to happen, I might have volunteered to be a guardian myself."

"I doubt you'd still have anyone living with you."

"Young people value their independence. I understand."

"Young people are morons," I said, which made him chuckle softly. "I'm serious. I'm talking about myself, too. We're stupid. We do stupid shit, and then when it comes back to bite us, we're surprised. We shouldn't be." My throat was tightening dangerously. I swallowed and tried to compose myself. "I don't want Viktor to be in here any more than you do. But C-Roy's not going to let us just walk out of here. Even if *you* ask nicely."

"Why do you say that?"

I shook my head and bit my lip.

"Croydon's a reasonable young man, Léa. And far more mature than many of the youngsters in town."

"Seriously? He's a dumbass frat boy."

"He's trying to hold on to power. One way to do that is with popularity. Or at least the appearance of it. He needs people to like him."

I frowned. "You make him sound insecure."

"Isn't he?"

"Not that I remember."

He swivelled a little in his chair. "You probably know him better than I do. What do you think he's going to do? Would he really deny Viktor a chance to get the care he needs?"

"I don't know," I said, but then I sighed. "No. He's not cruel."

"No. He's not."

"I just . . . I promised Viktor I wouldn't leave him. If I break that promise now, after everything that's happened—"

"So go with him."

"I can't."

"Why not?"

I shook my head. "There's nothing for me out there."

He smiled softly. "Viktor will be out there."

I turned my head away so I wouldn't have to look at him. "I don't want to give him the wrong idea. Besides, when this is over, when he's had more time to think about what happened . . ."

"What?" He placed his hand on my back. It was all I could do to keep from crying.

"He's going to blame me."

"Why?" he asked, sounding utterly confused. "You didn't do that to his eye, did you?"

"No. But I put him in that situation. He didn't want to be there. I was just so hungry . . . I wasn't thinking clearly, and now Viktor is fucking blind, and I—" The sob snuck out before I could stop it. I held my breath, certain there were more to follow.

"Léa, there's no shame in being hungry. And I'm sure you didn't force him to do anything. He was just trying to help you, the same way you helped him by getting him to me. That's what friends do."

Friends don't get their friends blinded by Rift energy, I thought miserably. I didn't dare speak. At last, I heard Dr. Bryan sigh. His hand left my back.

"We can talk more about that later. In the meantime, I need to get him upstairs." He stood up. "I want to make sure he doesn't wake up and try to walk around on his own. He's going to be woozy for a while yet." There was a pause. "Do you want to see him?"

I lifted my head and let my feet slide onto the floor. Nodding, I stood up. Dr. Bryan held out his hand as if he wanted me to walk ahead of him. But I hung back, and, eventually, he took the lead. I shuffled slowly after him, hugging myself.

Viktor was still stretched out on the table, just the way I'd left him, his legs dangling over one end. To my great relief, Dr. Bryan had cleaned everything up; there wasn't a trace of what had happened there, other than what was on his shirt. A pristine square of gauze was taped over Viktor's right eye—or, where his right eye had been. He looked a little too peaceful lying there. His head was turned to the side, and his mouth was slightly open, letting out a trickle of drool. Dr. Bryan grabbed some tissues from the box at the side of the room and quickly mopped up the spit.

"That's normal, by the way," he said, tossing the tissues into a nearby trash can.

"He doesn't usually drool in his sleep."

"I meant it's normal with sedation." Laying his hand gently on Viktor's hair, he leaned closer. "Viktor? Can you hear me?"

"Mm."

"I'll take that as a yes." He rubbed his shoulder. "My table's not very comfortable. Let's get you upstairs, all right?"

"Mm." Viktor's cloudy eye opened slowly. Dr. Bryan moved into his line of vision. Or what little was left.

"Do you think you can walk if Léa and I help you?"

"Charity," he mumbled.

Dr. Bryan chuckled. I frowned.

"What's he talking about?"

"Probably nothing. That's normal, too." He slipped his hand under Viktor's shoulder. "Come on. Up you get." He helped him sit up. Viktor wavered there for a moment, blinking his cloudy eye.

"Léa?"

"I'm here," I said quickly. He turned his head in my direction, but I knew by his blank expression that he couldn't really see me. I was probably nothing but a shadow.

He was actually steadier on his feet than I would've

thought. With me on one side and Dr. Bryan on the other, we steered him to the back of the clinic and through a door that led to a cramped vestibule with another door and a flight of stairs. The stairs weren't wide enough for all three of us at once, so Dr. Bryan had me run up ahead and open the door at the top while he helped Viktor make the climb.

The apartment wasn't what I was expecting. Maybe I'd just lived in the Rift Zone for too long amongst so much brokenness. Dr. Bryan's place looked like something from outside the Zone . . . or at least from pre-Rift Kenyonville. There obviously wasn't any air-conditioning because all the windows were open, but the apartment wasn't uncomfortably warm, either. The living area was a cozy space with a small couch, an easy chair, a fireplace with a mantel covered in half-melted candles, and a couple of book-cases stuffed full of neatly arranged books. Framed artwork hung on the walls. It all looked overly clean and tidy, like the place had been staged for an open house.

"It's a good thing I made my bed this morning," Dr. Bryan said, drawing my attention back to him as he disappeared with Viktor through a doorway off to the left. I followed, just in time to see him help Viktor sit down on the edge of a single bed. "You're probably a little tall for these accommodations, but it's either this or the couch. It'll be quieter in here."

Viktor nodded. He seemed to be a little less groggy

than he was even a few minutes earlier. Reaching up, he gingerly touched the gauze pad.

"You just had surgery. Do you remember?"

He nodded again, dropping his hand and bowing his head. Dr. Bryan crouched down in front of him.

"It went well. There were no complications. Keep the wound clean, and you'll heal."

Viktor didn't say anything. Dr. Bryan watched him for a few moments, then turned his attention downward.

"Let's get your boots off. Then you can rest. I'll get something for you and Léa to eat, and we'll talk about the next steps. All right?"

When Viktor didn't respond at all, Dr. Bryan glanced at me. I didn't know what to say. I didn't know what to do. I was so tired. Tired of the situation. Tired of that day. Tired of the Zone.

When Viktor's boots were off and he was sprawled out on the bed, his feet dangling over the end, Dr. Bryan edged out of the room, leaning close to me as he passed.

"Talk to him," he said softly. I turned to him with a frown.

"He doesn't want to talk."

"Then *you* talk." He patted my shoulder and walked into the kitchen. I turned back to the boy on the bed.

"Viktor," I whispered. There was no response. I stepped into the room. My sneakers sounded loud on the wooden floor, so I slipped them off and padded to the bed in my bare feet. As if he could sense my presence, he rolled onto his side, away from me. "Can I sit with you?"

He didn't answer. I settled myself on the edge of the bed. There wasn't a lot of room, so I was careful when I lay down, lest I fall on the floor. The ceiling above me was textured, like the ceiling in my old bedroom. I looked away, turning my head to look at Viktor's back. That's when I noticed the shaking. Except it wasn't just shaking. It was crying.

I rolled toward him and curled my body against his, wrapping my arm around his shoulders. He sucked in a shuddering breath.

"Talk to me," I whispered. "Please. I don't want to remember your last words as 'fuck that.' That's not who you are."

He jerked like he was hiccuping. "You have no idea who I am," he said, startling me with the first sentence I'd heard from him in hours. His voice was raspy, as if he'd screamed it raw. I held my breath, waiting to see if he would go on. When he didn't, though, I pulled myself closer.

"Then tell me."

He took a deep breath. "My name is Cody."

CHAPTER 12

CODY LAMOREAUX AND THE SCIENCE PROJECT OF DOOM

"She was right," Viktor said, confusing me with a rapid subject change right after his revelation.

"Who?"

"Charity."

"Who's Charity?"

"Rasputin. Charity and Loyal Sutton."

"You know them?"

"I didn't think she'd—" He broke off, his voice catching. I held him a little tighter.

"Why didn't you say something before you got in that chair?"

"I didn't think she recognized me. It's been three years. I look different now." He pulled up his hands to cover his face. "How bad is it?"

"How bad is what?"

"Do I have a massive hole in my face?"

"I . . . haven't seen it."

He was crying again. I could feel it, even if I couldn't hear it.

"Viktor—"

"It's Cody. Cody Lamoreaux. I'm eighteen, not seventeen. And Ramona's not my cousin."

"Then who is she?"

"My sister." He let out a sob that shook us both. "I'm sorry!"

"For what?" I asked. It certainly didn't seem like he should've been the one apologizing for anything at that moment.

"I lied."

"Why?"

"To protect my family. To protect myself. I made a mistake, and—" His breath hitched. "I'm sorry."

I shook my head. "Why did you have to lie?"

"Because I caused the Rift."

I blinked as a strange chill slipped through my veins and down my arms. It almost felt like my hands were going to flare. Luckily, they didn't. "Doing what?"

"My science project. I don't even know what happened. Marc was using the same power supply on the bench and—"

"Permanent Marc?"

"The Rift tore a hole in the middle of the science lab. I don't know how . . . There was this pink flash . . ." He grabbed the arm I had draped around his shoulders with both hands. I could feel the desperation in his fingertips as they dug into my forearm. "It doesn't matter what happened. Everybody knew it was me. By the time I got home that night, they were already there. Waiting."

"Who was?"

"I don't know. That's the whole point of people like that. They'd already seized my project. Then they said that Cody had to disappear."

"Disappear?" The word made me shudder.

"They created a new identity: Viktor Knowles. A fourteen-year-old child genius who'd lost his parents in a car accident and had gone to live with his aunt and uncle in Kenyonville, just days before the Rift happened."

"So what happened to Cody?"

"Officially, he died. Exposure to the Rift. He was the closest, so it was logical. Remember the shrine? That wasn't for some cousin. That was for Cody. It's all part of the official story. The official lie."

I didn't say anything. I didn't know *what* to say. The flood of secrets, borne by his desperate words, filled the quiet room. There were so many questions I wanted to ask, but I could sense something odd in his body, a sort of electric tremble that made me suspect he was right on the edge. It didn't feel like anything to do with the Rift. This was something that ran deeper. Something that came from a very dark place. And this was Viktor we were talking about . . . so it just felt wrong.

"Charity was right," he said, his voice barely a

murmur. "Everything that's happened in the Rift Zone . . . Every person who's died . . . That's on me."

"No, it's—"

"It is."

"But how did a high school science project cause the Rift? How do you know it was something you did?"

"I was right there. I saw the flash. What else would it have been?"

I didn't have an answer to that question.

"It was my fault. When I burned my face, I figured it was karma. Just a little payback for what I'd done. I didn't realize—" His voice tightened so much he had to stop and take a deep breath. "I didn't realize the punishment wasn't over yet."

"Viktor. No."

"It's better this way. I'll never be able to create another Rift and destroy a whole town."

"You don't deserve this."

"Yes, I do. I deserve all of this and more. Look at everything that's happened to us in this heckhole. You lost a toe . . . and whatever else you're not telling me about. Niesha lost her house. Click got stuck here, and he's probably never going to see his family again. Buddy had to eat his owner's face to survive." He shook his head slowly on the pillow. "Then there're all the others. Charity and Loyal. Dr. Frazier. Carrick. Everyone's lost something, and they lost it because of me. If I have to spend the rest of my life blind and disfigured, it's only a *fraction* of what I deserve."

The self-hatred rolling off of him was palpable. I wanted to pull away, to get away from the vile energy of it, but I knew I couldn't. The Rift had torn a hole through our town—and our lives—but I wasn't ready to condemn him for it.

"You didn't do it on purpose, did you?"

"It doesn't matter." He choked on a sob. "It doesn't matter, Léa. It's done. I can't go back. None of us can."

The room fell silent. I leaned my head forward, resting it against the back of his. His hair smelled fresh, almost dewy, and I remembered the diffuser in the Smile & Shine office. The reminder of what was probably the worst day of his life clung to him, making it impossible to let him forget.

—

Viktor refused to eat, but Dr. Bryan did convince him to sip on a glass of water with electrolyte mix. I perched on the edge of the bed, nursing a tiny amount of fruit cocktail in a bowl that made the portion look ridiculously small. But I wasn't about to push it; I hadn't eaten properly in weeks, and I didn't want to get sick and puke up valuable food. So I ate each piece one at a time, savouring the flavours of the syrupy peaches, grainy pears, stringy pineapple chunks, and spongy cherries. Dr. Bryan left us alone, perhaps sensing that we needed time to process things on our own.

When Viktor had downed half the glass of pale yellow drink, he handed the rest to me and curled up on the bed again. I drank it down, trying to ignore the chalky lemon flavour, before taking the empty dishes to the kitchen.

Dr. Bryan was sitting in the easy chair. I wasn't sure if he was just pretending to read, or if he really was interested in the hardcover splayed open on his lap. There was no dishwasher in the tiny kitchen, so I rinsed out the dishes with hot water and left them in the sink. As I turned off the water, I thought I heard a voice. I paused, hand on the faucet, and listened. But all I could hear was the turning of a book page and the soft hum of the fridge. I quickly dried my hands on the towel that hung on the oven door, then walked into the living room. Dr. Bryan looked up.

"How's he doing?"

I shrugged and flopped onto the couch. Then I realized how grubby I was, and I stood up again. Dr. Bryan raised an eyebrow.

"Are you all right?"

"I don't want to get your couch dirty."

He grunted in amusement. "It's not as clean as it looks. It's probably older than you, and it was the favourite spot of two rather large dogs." He waved his hand. "Sit down. It's fine."

I sat gingerly. His expression darkened as he peered at my face.

"I might have some antibiotic cream for that. You

really should put something on it. It looks like it's starting to blister."

"I don't care."

"Well, I do. If you get an infection on my watch, I'd be a lousy doctor."

"You're a vet."

"So? You're an animal. The mechanisms of a burn are the same, whether you have feathers or fur."

I gave him a funny look.

"Obviously, you have neither. You know what I mean." He closed his book and left it on his lap. "We should talk about the next steps. Once Viktor's gotten some rest, I really think you should—" He broke off. I wasn't sure why . . . until I heard what he obviously had.

"Lee-ah!"

I sprang from the couch and hurried to the open window. As I grasped the sill and peered down, I saw Click looking back up at me. When he saw me, his face broke into a huge grin.

"Oh, my god," I breathed, pulling back inside. I sprinted to the door, flew down the stairs, and ran back through the clinic. The tile floor felt cold under my bare feet, and I realized I'd forgotten my shoes. I didn't care. I fumbled with the lock before throwing open the door. "Where have you been?" I shouted.

Click's eyes widened, and he took a step back. I probably looked like a crazy person coming at him like that. I slowed to a stop, mindful of the rough sidewalk under my bare soles. Buddy trotted out from around a corner, and I whirled on him, a sudden fury making me see literal redness.

"Bad dog!" I shouted, taking a step in his direction. He skittered away, ears back, and tried to hide behind Click's legs. "Bad!"

"Lee-ah," Click said. He took a step forward, his hand stretched toward my face. I smacked it away.

"Viktor's hurt. And you were just chasing that stupid—" I broke off as he raised his hand to my face again. His fingers hovered just above the burn, not quite touching. "It's fine. Viktor's worse."

He closed his eyes but kept his hand where it was. I frowned as I felt something . . . soft. I knew he wasn't actually touching the burn—because that would've hurt like a bitch—but there was this warm, almost fluffy sensation that felt like a caress. My mind skipped back to another time and place, and I remembered sitting on the grass in the park with what I'd thought was a broken ankle. His non-touch had felt nice then, too.

"What are you doing? Reiki?"

He took a deep, relaxed breath and let it out slowly on a nearly imperceptible hum. I suddenly felt drowsy, and my eyelids drooped.

"Lee-ah," Click said. I opened my eyes, blinking, completely disoriented. When I looked down, Buddy wasn't cowering behind his friend anymore. He was lying on the sidewalk in a patch of shade, patiently waiting.

"What did you do?" My hand rose to my cheek, even as my brain screamed out a warning. But all my fingers encountered was smooth, slightly sticky skin. New skin. I dropped my hand and stared at the boy in front of me, my eyes so wide it almost hurt. "Did you just *heal* it?"

When he gave me a thumbs up, my brain stuttered as the puzzle pieces clattered into place.

"You healed my ankle before, too, didn't you? That's why there was a past break on the x-ray."

He blinked his golden eyes at me, a little smile playing on his features.

"Where were you?" I screamed, so suddenly that he flinched. Buddy bolted halfway down the block. But I wasn't done. "Viktor needed you! You could've saved— You could've— He wouldn't have lost—"

"Léa! What's going on?"

The sound of Dr. Bryan's voice cut through my fog of rage. And it was a good thing, too, because I was so close to grabbing Click by his denim jacket and shaking him until his teeth broke. I whirled around to face the vet, who blinked in confusion.

"What . . . ?" he asked.

"It doesn't matter! It's too late. All because that *stupid* dog"—I waved my hand at the scruffy white thing that was cowering near the corner of the building—"had to run off. Niesha warned us about having a dog in the Zone, but did we listen? No. Stupid little piece of—"

"Léa, he's a dog. And, right now, you're scaring him."

"If it wasn't for that stupid dog, Viktor would still be able to see."

Dr. Bryan shook his head. "It couldn't be saved. The damage was too severe."

"What do you think this is?" I asked, tapping my cheekbone. It didn't even hurt.

He stepped closer and peered at my face, running his thumb just under the healed area. "I've never seen anything like it." He shook his head and turned to Click. "Did you do this?"

Click gave him a thumbs up. But he didn't look so sure now.

"Incredible."

"It's not incredible," I said, nearly spitting the words. "If Viktor finds out you didn't have to cut out his eye—"

"So we won't tell him," he said, just as Click jerked and blurted out, "Vee-kah."

I shook my head. "It's too late."

Click pointed to his right eye. When I shook my head, he let his hand drop. He seemed to understand . . . and the devastated expression on his face said it all.

"Come inside," Dr. Bryan said, holding out a hand and beckoning to me and Click. "I'm sure Viktor would like to see you."

"He can't see anything," I snapped. I stormed back to the clinic door and yanked it open. As I walked back inside, I could hear the vet's soft voice behind me. My feet smacked on the cool floor as I walked back to the stairs, then thumped on the carpeted treads as I stomped my way up. *Calm down*, I told myself. *The last thing Viktor needs right now is a bitchy companion.* I walked back to the bedroom, only to come to a quick stop in the doorway. The bed was empty.

His boots were still there, though. I peered down the short hallway, noting the closed door at the end. Now that I thought about it, I kind of had to pee myself. But I would just have to wait my turn.

Dr. Bryan's arrival was announced by the telltale sound of flip-flops. Click followed hesitantly, Buddy in his arms. The dog looked a little more relaxed now (probably because I wasn't yelling at him), but he was furiously sniffing the air as if trying to gather all the information he could about this new environment he'd found himself in.

"Vee-kah," Click said to me. I waved my hand toward the bathroom. He frowned.

"I'm going next, so don't get any ideas about cutting in line."

His frown deepened. "Vee-kah."

"He's in the bathroom."

Click deposited Buddy on the floor. The dog shook himself out, then trotted off to explore. Click stood there for a moment, then turned toward the bedroom.

I wasn't sure if he could smell that Viktor had been in there or not. I wouldn't have been surprised. We were all getting kind of ripe. But the boy wasn't looking at the bed or at the boots sitting beside it. He crossed the room and peered out the window. This one was on the back of the building, and it faced west. Through it, I could see the deepening grey of the sky. There was no vivid sunset that night. Just a dull expanse that signalled the end of a terrible day.

Click didn't seem to care about the sunset (or lack thereof), though. He wasn't looking at the sky. His attention was focused lower, at something on the ground. I tiptoed into the room and went to join him at the window. At first, I couldn't see much in the shadowy laneway. But then something flared pink. Two somethings.

"Oh, my god. No."

CHAPTER 13

PINKHANDS

My incoherent screams echoed around me as I flew down the stairs and wrenched open the door at the back of the little vestibule. I stumbled out into the twilight, tripped on the discarded jeans and t-shirt, and sprawled onto my knees. I felt no pain. There was too much adrenaline for that. My screams bounced off the buildings around us, but they didn't seem to faze the naked boy standing just feet away, his head tilted back toward the sky, each hand filled with pink flames that flared and wavered and made the alleyway look like it was lit by a kawaii campfire. But there was nothing cute about what he was going to do.

"Stop!" I screamed, finally able to form my terror into a single word. I stood up and barreled forward, smacking into him from behind so hard that he stumbled. Luckily, we didn't go down.

"Let go." His voice was flat.

"Stop!"

"Let me go."

"No! I'm not going to let you do this." I held on tight, my arms wrapped around his body. He was trembling, but he wasn't cold. If anything, he felt hot. Feverish.

"Léa, it's over."

"It's not!" I shouted. I turned my head to the side, spotting his left hand, which he was holding a little farther from his body now. "It's only over if you give up."

"Let go. Please."

"No! Do you really want to end up like Carrick?"

"I won't."

"Yes, you will. You'll live in agony, and then you'll die." I tightened my arms. "You'll die."

"Maybe that's what I want!" he shouted. "Maybe that's what I deserve!"

"Not like that."

"Exactly like that." His body hitched as he tried to suppress a sob. "But I'm not taking you with me, so you have to let go."

"No."

"Let go!" he screamed. I felt the raw anguish of his voice vibrate through our bodies.

"Vee-kah," a voice said, and the next thing I felt was Click's embrace as he reached around both of us from the front. Viktor's body shuddered, and his legs seemed to wobble. I held on tight.

"The Viktor I know wouldn't do this to his friends," I said, pressing my forehead against his too-hot skin.

"You don't know me. Viktor doesn't even exist."

"Yes, he does. He's an annoying doofus with questionable hygiene and a penchant for fart noises. But he's also a sweet guy who tries to look on the bright side, even when things are at their shittiest. He cares so much about his friends that he makes them eat pine trees just so they won't starve to death. He's the only good thing about this fucking hellhole, and if he kills himself and takes away that one good thing, I'll never forgive him."

There was silence in the alley. I turned my head and pressed my ear against his back as I closed my eyes. I could hear someone's heart thumping—it might've been either of ours—and the sound felt reassuring. Life still existed in that alleyway.

"If you were the terrible person you think you are," I said, "you would have done it already. You would have burned me and Click, too. But you haven't. Because you're not that person."

"You don't know—"

"Yes, I do. I don't care what happened before. I don't care who you were then. I care about who you are now."

His knees buckled. I still had my arms wrapped around him, and so did Click, but that wasn't enough to stop the collapse. We all went down as one, onto the gritty pavement. Into the shadows. Viktor's hands were no longer glowing. He pressed them over his face as he slumped in my arms and started to sob.

"Vee-kah," Click said, leaning down to try to look into his face. He brushed a few strands of dark hair back, then rested his fingers on Viktor's right hand and closed his eyes. In my arms, Viktor slowly seemed to relax. His bunched muscles softened. The trembling faded. The sobs tapered off.

"I'm sorry," he whispered, letting his hands fall away from his face. "I just keep hurting you, don't I?"

"It's okay." I let my chin rest on his shoulder for a moment.

"No, it's not."

"Okay, it's not. But I understand."

"Do you?"

I frowned and looked at Click. His expression seemed to mirror mine. I didn't know what else to say. Viktor was right. I didn't understand. I could imagine what he was going through . . . but that wasn't really the same thing.

A smack of flip-flops alerted me to Dr. Bryan's approach. I looked up to find him standing there, holding Viktor's clothes. I wasn't sure how much he'd seen or heard, but, judging by the sad expression on his face, it was safe to say that he'd probably witnessed most of it. He crouched down beside Click and laid a gentle hand on Viktor's hair.

"It's going to get chilly out here. Let's get your clothes back on and head upstairs."

—

Dr. Bryan got Viktor dressed, and then he guided him back up the stairs, into the apartment, and to the bedroom. The boy collapsed on the bed, utterly spent. He curled up on his side, closing his remaining eye against the rapidly fading light from the window. When he was settled, Dr. Bryan gave me a pointed look. I nodded.

"Click's going to stay with you, okay?"

Viktor didn't acknowledge me, but Click gave me a thumbs up before going and settling himself on the floor beside the cast-off boots. Buddy joined him. I turned back to the vet and followed him out of the bedroom.

"Do you know where Croydon lives?" he asked quietly when we were sitting in the living room in the warm glow of the lamp in the corner.

"Yeah. As long as he hasn't moved in the last year."

He shook his head. "I doubt it." He looked down at his shirt and seemed to notice the flecks of blood for the first time. Frowning, he scratched at them with a fingernail. "We'll leave tomorrow. After you three have gotten some proper rest and had something to eat."

"No."

He stopped playing with Viktor's blood and looked up. "No?"

I shook my head. "You're not coming with us."

His eyebrows rose. "And why would that be?"

"Because we're in the Rift Zone, and you're . . ."

"Old?" he offered.

"I was going to say you're not a Rifter. But that works, too."

"I may not be a Rifter, but I still want to help."

"You already have."

"Léa, I'm not going to let you kids—"

"I'm twenty. Viktor's seventeen. You're not obligated to do anything to help us."

"I know that. But I still want to."

I nodded. "Write a note to C-Roy. But you're not coming with us."

"Why not?" he demanded. It struck me as weird. Somehow, it seemed like it should've been me, the relative child, begging to go on the expedition. But the roles were reversed. I wasn't sure I liked that.

In answer to his question, I lifted my hand and let it flare. The pink lit up the space like a decorative lamp. I could see the dancing energy reflected in his eyes. "This is why. You can't protect yourself against this."

"I'll be with you."

"Not on the way back."

He frowned. "You're not coming back with me?"

I shook my head, then shook my hand, letting the pink go out. "We can't ask you to take us in."

"You're not. I'm offering."

"You don't have enough food to split three ways."

"Then I'll make an arrangement with Croydon so that I do."

With a sigh, I folded my arms and sank back into the couch. "He's not going to go for that."

"I think you'd be surprised, Léa."

I think you'd be surprised, too, I thought. But I didn't say anything out loud. I knew exactly how this interaction with C-Roy was going to go. That was one of the reasons I didn't want Dr. Bryan coming with us. He probably wouldn't approve of what I was going to have to do.

"Do you think you can handle Viktor by yourself?" he asked.

"Click will help. And I know where we're going, so it's not like we're going to get lost."

He shook his head. "I don't like the idea of letting you go off by yourselves. Especially with Viktor . . ."

I nodded. I knew what he meant. But we didn't really have much of a choice. What was done was done. And if Viktor was going to have any chance at a decent life, he needed to get out of the Zone. Away from the Rift. Back to civilization, where he could get the help he needed.

"You can go with him, Léa."

I looked up into the vet's face. He stared back intently, his eyebrows raised. "Maybe," I said.

That seemed to satisfy him. Which was good, because I didn't feel like having to defend my actual plans.

A huge yawn snuck out before I could stop it. Dr. Bryan grunted.

"Get some rest. I've got some extra blankets in the linen cupboard, and you can use the couch."

"It's okay." I stood up. "I can share with Viktor. I'm used to the stink."

He chuckled. "You're all welcome to use the shower before you go."

"Thanks. I might take you up on it. But don't count on Viktor going anywhere near a bar of soap."

He smiled, so I edged around the couch and headed for the bathroom. The fruit salad and electrolyte drink seemed to have kicked my urinary system into gear, and now I really had to pee. I did that, then washed my hands. The mirror above the sink showed a tired-looking girl with dark circles under her eyes. I tilted my head, examining the healed burn. The skin was pink and smooth. It would probably heal without any sort of scar.

I finished up in the bathroom, then headed to the bedroom. Click was curled up on the floor, dog at his side, already fast asleep. Viktor was still, too, his breathing deep and even. I carefully crawled onto the bed and settled myself behind him, effectively creating a barrier between him and the door. If he tried to get off the other side of the bed, he'd step on Click. In any case, he wouldn't be able to sneak out and try to end things before we had a chance to stop him. Gently, I rested my hand on his shoulder. He felt hot, even through his t-shirt, and when I moved my hand down past his sleeve, I could feel the sweaty feverishness of his skin.

I didn't want to let him go. But Dr. Bryan was right. He needed more than what we could give him in the Rift Zone.

I just hoped he would accept the help he needed.

CHAPTER 14

THE DAY AFTER

Sharing a single bed with a fully grown guy (even one as skinny as Viktor) wasn't the easiest thing. I didn't get much sleep at all. He didn't, either. Every time I woke up from my shattered dreaming, I could sense that he was awake beside me. He never said a word, but I could tell.

By the time a dull light started filtering through the window, I was more exhausted than when I'd lain down. I was on my back, staring up at the ceiling. So was Viktor. When I turned to look at him, I saw that his eye was open. Hesitantly, I reached up and brushed the backs of my fingers over his lumpy scar.

"You should've let me do it," he whispered. I didn't have to ask what he meant.

"Would you have let me do that to myself?"

He chewed on his lip for a moment. "You don't need to be punished."

"Fuck, Viktor. Neither do you."

"I destroyed a whole town."

"On purpose?"

"No, but—"

"No buts. Intention counts for something." I frowned as I thought about what he'd already told me . . . and what he hadn't. "What was this science project, anyway?"

His chin trembled. "Cymatic resonance for accelerated wound healing."

"What's that?"

"Using sound frequencies to make wounds heal faster."

My fingers hesitated against his scarred cheek. "You built a healing machine?"

He sighed and closed his eye. "You don't have to keep your promise."

"What promise?"

"You said you wouldn't leave me. But I'm not going to hold you to it. You don't have to be the Antigone to my Oedipus."

I frowned and pulled my hand away from his cheek. "Huh?"

"She led a blind guy around." He shook his head slowly on the pillow. "Never mind."

I wiggled around and propped myself up on one elbow so I could see him better. "Then what do you suggest?"

"I don't know. Just . . . not that." He nibbled on his

bottom lip for a moment before taking a deep breath. "I know I'll get used to it. I'll have to. It's just . . ."

"I know."

His lip trembled. "I should've built a time machine for my science project instead."

"You know how to build a time machine?"

"No. But I obviously didn't know what I was doing with what I did build." He took a shaky breath. "I guess I wouldn't need the time machine if I hadn't built that thing, anyway."

"What would you have gone back and changed?"

"I would've built a time machine instead."

I let out a soft snort. "So you could go back and change the outcome that wouldn't have needed changing."

"If I had one now, I would just use it to go back to yesterday. Before . . ." He trailed off, the devastation evident in his choked voice.

"I know."

He opened his eye and turned his head in my direction.

"Can you see me?" I asked.

He shook his head. "There's not enough light in here. All I can see are shadows." He lifted his hand toward me. I caught it and wrapped my fingers around his. "I don't know if I can do this," he whispered. "We have no home. No alliances. If anything happens to you and Click because I can't—"

"We're fine," I said, giving his hand a squeeze. "I

survived in the Rift Zone for almost two years by myself."

"You lost a toe."

"Thanks for reminding me." I studied his face, not sure if he was just pointing out an inconvenient fact or if he was teasing me. I really hoped it was the latter. "And that had nothing to do with being alone. I wasn't alone."

He blinked. "Are you finally going to tell me what happened?"

"The story's not that exciting."

"But it's about you. So I want to hear it."

I felt my cheeks go red. Selfishly, I was glad he couldn't see them. "I was working with C-Roy's crew. We were trying to get into a safe in one of those swanky houses down in southeast Kenyonville."

"A heist?"

I snorted. "Hardly. Just a bunch of teenagers who didn't know what the fuck they were doing. None of us could crack the safe, so someone got the bright idea that we'd dig it out of the wall and take it back to C-Roy's."

"How does that help get it open?"

"It doesn't. And I pointed that out. But those idiots thought that, if they had enough time, someone would be able to get it open."

"So how did that lead to nine toes?"

I looked down at my bare feet. My right foot was tucked under the left, pressed against the bedspread, so I couldn't see the missing toe. I could feel it, though. Talking about it seemed to be making the phantom sensation worse. "I got too close. They were moving it with a dolly, and everybody had to help to keep it steady. We still almost bent the damn dolly. We were going down some steps, and the guy doing the steering lost control. I tried to jump out of the way, but I wasn't fast enough. The safe fell off the dolly and the corner smashed my toe."

"Spit," he whispered, which made me smile a little. I was just glad he was starting to sound like Viktor again. "What did you do?"

"Nothing, at first. Hobbled home. But someone told C-Roy, and he had me hauled off to Dr. Bryan."

"And the doc cut it off."

"It wasn't really a toe anymore. At least, that's what I've been told."

His hand tightened on mine. His skin felt warmer than ever. I pulled my hand away and laid it on his forehead. He flinched a little at the touch he hadn't seen coming.

"Sorry," I said, frowning as I let my hand linger there. "You're so hot."

He opened his mouth, and I held my breath, hoping to hear the quick-witted reply that I'd set him up for. Instead, though, his forehead crumpled under my hand. "I just wish I could see your face, Léa. One last time."

I didn't want to unpack those words. I didn't want

to tell him what Dr. Bryan and I had planned, either. I had a feeling he wasn't going to go along with it. Not without a fight. And I didn't want to fight with him in our last few hours together. So I just lay down beside him, snuggling up against his side, and rested my hand on his chest. He took in a surprised breath.

"Is this okay?" I whispered. "If it makes you too warm, I can—"

"No. Stay." He reached up and placed his hand over mine. "Thank you."

I closed my eyes and rested my chin on his shoulder. Maybe I was giving him the wrong idea.

Maybe I was just tired of fighting it.

—

The next time I opened my eyes, the room was a lot brighter. I had to pee again, so some time must have passed. I rubbed the sleep from my eyes as I rolled onto my back. And that's when I felt the emptiness of the bed.

I sat up like a shot. From that angle, I could see that the floor was empty, too. The boy and the dog were no longer curled up there. My heart started to calm down a little. By the time I walked into the living room and spotted the three figures sitting there, relief had taken over . . . and the urge to pee was almost overwhelming. I made a quick detour to the bathroom.

When I came out again, Dr. Bryan was in the

kitchen. I went and sat down next to Viktor on the couch. The heat radiating off of him was even more intense than it had been a few hours earlier.

"Are you okay?" I asked.

"Who? Me?"

"Yes, you."

His lips twisted in an expression that was halfway between a smirk and a grimace. "Am I supposed to be?"

I looked up at Dr. Bryan, who was approaching with a glass in one hand and a plate in the other. He handed both to me, then went to sit down in the armchair. I frowned down at the glass (which obviously held more of that electrolyte drink) and the plate (which held two crackers smeared with what looked like peanut butter).

"You don't have a peanut allergy, do you?" he asked.

"No. But there are more than two of us."

He chuckled. "We already ate, Léa."

"Hours ago," Viktor said, a small smile playing on his lips. "Had to let you get your beauty sleep."

I balanced the plate on my lap while I drank half the liquid. "It didn't work. I look like shit."

His smile died. I quickly turned to Dr. Bryan.

"I think he's got a fever."

"He does."

"So? Can't you do something about it?"

He shook his head. "It's not the fever I'm worried about. It's what's causing it."

"And that is . . . ?"

"An infection," Viktor said. He scratched at the skin around the tape.

"It's not uncommon," Dr. Bryan said. "Considering the circumstances. But I'm all out of antibiotics at the moment."

I stared at Viktor, then turned back to the vet. He must've seen something in my expression, because he quickly shook his head.

"It's not that bad. Yet. But he definitely needs some antibiotics if we're going to keep any infections in check." He leaned forward and gave me a pointed look. "Croydon can get what I need."

"Oh," I said. "*Oh,*" I repeated when I understood what he was getting at. "You want me to go get them for you?"

"I do. It's not safe for an old guy like me out there. I don't have the built-in weaponry."

I snorted, hoping I was keeping things just light enough that Viktor would buy the ruse. The vet probably knew that, if we told Viktor about the plan to banish him from the Rift Zone (for his own good, of course), it wasn't going to go over very well.

"It's not all it's cracked up to be," Viktor muttered.

"What isn't?" Dr. Bryan asked.

"Don't ask—" I began, just as Viktor let out a raspberry and let his left hand flare. Dr. Bryan actually jumped.

"Impressive."

"But dangerous," I said, staring at the menace flickering over Viktor's skin. He appeared to be staring at it, too, his brow creased in concentration.

"Can you see that?" Dr. Bryan asked. Viktor nodded, then quickly squeezed his fingers into a fist. It looked like he'd just crushed a juicy pink fruit in his hand.

"Just barely. That'll be terribly useful."

Dr. Bryan nodded. "It's a good sign, though. It means the damage to that eye isn't as severe. It's probably limited to the cornea."

I shot him a quick look and shook my head. He glanced at me, then turned back to Viktor.

"Maybe one day," Viktor said, "when this is all over . . ." He trailed off and sighed. "That's what we were saying three years ago, though. I better get used to being blind."

Dr. Bryan and I exchanged another look. This time, Click noticed. He'd been sitting cross-legged on the floor, gently stroking his fingers through Buddy's scruffy fur, just listening. But now he was fully alert. And he knew something was up.

"I'm going with you to C-Roy's," Viktor said. My heart surged, but I tried to remain calm.

"You think that's a good idea?"

"I think backup is always a good idea."

"So I'll take Click."

He shook his head. "Click's not a Rifter. No offence," he said, directing his words in Click's direction. Sort of.

"So you're going to lob Riftballs at someone you can't see?"

"I'm a deterrent." He sat up a little straighter. "Plus, I could be a cautionary tale."

"What?"

"If anyone asks what happened to me, we'll tell them you burned my eyes out with Rift energy. That should keep the crazies at bay."

"Yeah, and paint me as completely batshit."

"Good. Who'd mess with a batspit Rifter like that?"

I let out a sigh. Half of it was relief. He'd walked right into the plan, just like we'd hoped. "Fine. You can come. But Click's coming, too." I glanced over at Click. He gave me a bemused thumbs up. "Okay. He's in."

"That's settled, then," Dr. Bryan said. He glanced at Click, then gave me a quick wink. I pretended I hadn't noticed.

I ate my two peanut butter crackers slowly, sipping on the rest of the drink between bites. Click kept staring at me like he wanted a better explanation. But I couldn't very well say anything with Viktor sitting right there. Besides, I didn't know how he was going to react. He loved Viktor; I had no idea what he was going to do when he found out his friend was going away.

When I was done eating, I took my dishes to the sink, just as Dr. Bryan said he wanted to check Viktor's wound. Without saying a word to anyone, I practically ran for the bathroom, stripped off my clothes, and hopped into the shower. It was as good an excuse as any. Really, though, I just didn't want to see what was under that gauze.

—

We left just after noon. Dr. Bryan helped Viktor down the stairs, and then I took over, leading him through the clinic and out the door onto Main Street. The day had started out bright, and there were still patches of blue sky overhead, but there were also clouds moving in from the south. Grey ones.

"If you can't make it back before nightfall—or if it starts to rain—find shelter," Dr. Bryan said, fumbling in his pocket for something. He pulled out a folded piece of paper and handed it to me. "A list of what I need," he said. I opened it awkwardly with one hand and had a look. There was a list . . . but there was also a request:

Croydon,

This boy needs more medical attention than I can give him. I would appreciate it if you could render your specific brand of assistance.

Gratefully,
Sol Bryan, DVM

I frowned as I folded up the letter and stuck it in my jeans pocket. "Will he . . . understand what you need?"

"He should. I tried to make my handwriting as neat as possible. But you know us doctors."

Viktor turned his head in the vet's direction. "Spitty handwriting?"

"It's not the best."

"Neither is mine." He shrugged. "On the bright side, I guess I'll never have to write anything by hand again."

Dr. Bryan frowned. "I'm all for having realistic expectations, Viktor, but I don't think you should write off your vision so easily. Things could change."

I shot the vet a sharp look, which he didn't seem to notice. At my side, Viktor shook his head slowly.

"We might not get out of here for years if those donkeybutts at the checkpoints have anything to say about it." He adjusted his grip on my elbow and tried to look down at me. "We should go, Léa. I'm going to be slow, and I'd rather get you and Click back here before it gets dark."

I nodded, shooting a quick glance at Dr. Bryan, who returned the gesture. Tricking Viktor into getting help felt like a shitty thing to do . . . but I had a feeling it was the only way we were going to make it happen.

We set off, heading down Main Street until we got to Sandpiper Avenue, and then turned left. Viktor was slow, but he was trying really hard. I could tell by the way he clung to my elbow. His hand felt hot, even through my jacket sleeve, a continuous reminder of why we were heading back to a place I'd promised myself I would never return to. Click, seemingly unaware of the real reason for our journey, bounced along beside us, keeping close to Viktor while not quite touching him. Buddy trotted a little ahead, his tail bouncing like a white flag. It seemed fitting, somehow. I, at least, felt like I was surrendering to fate.

The area around Main Street was older. Renovated, yes, and perfectly welcoming to visitors (or, it had been, before the Rift), but still on the worn-in side of things. As we drew closer to the boundary between Ryver's and C-Roy's territories, there was a shift. The streets got curvier, and greener, with more gardens. Many of those were overgrown, but there were still a few that were being taken care of. Some people, at least, seemed to care what their surroundings looked like. Or maybe gardening was just a way to pass the time; there certainly wasn't much else to do for entertainment.

C-Roy lived almost smack in the middle of his territory. It was an upper middle-class sort of neighbourhood—not as swanky as the area to the southeast, but still pretty damn nice, considering the state of some of the other neighbourhoods in the Zone. I wondered if maybe Dr. Bryan was right about C-Roy's level of maturity. He was the oldest boss in town, and even though he presented himself as a party-boy moron, he had to have been doing something right, given the appearance of his territory. It made me wonder about who he *really* was. Who he had been, before all of this shit with the Rift had gone down.

As we stepped across the boundary (invisible as far as fences or markings went, but still really obvious due to the state of the properties), I was kind of glad Viktor wasn't able to see our surroundings. Not that I was happy about his injuries. But I knew that, if he could see what I'd left behind here, he would want to know why.

And I really didn't want to get into that.

—

C-Roy didn't see us coming. He was out in the front yard of his house, a blue saltbox with a bright yellow door, mowing the grass. Or, rather, he was fighting with the cord on the electric lawnmower, because it seemed to be tangled in the patch of garden in the middle of the lawn. Buddy caught his attention first, running onto the plush turf and throwing himself down to roll on his back. C-Roy quickly turned off the mower.

"Hey," I heard him say. "Where'd you come from?" He looked up and around. As soon as he spotted us, I felt my cheeks get red. I tried to keep my pace steady, though; I didn't want Viktor to sense my tension.

"Sorry," I called, waving my free hand toward the dog who was grinding his back into the freshly mowed grass.

"No problem. I was going to call it quits, anyway. I wanted to get this done before the rain started, but I don't think that's going to happen."

"What rain?" I asked, flinching as I felt a drop hit my cheek. C-Roy started to push the now-silent lawnmower back toward the detached garage. I steered Viktor in that direction, leading him up the slightly sloping driveway.

"It's been a while," C-Roy said as he unplugged the cord and began to wind it into a coil.

"A year." My voice was flat. I couldn't quite read him, and that made me nervous. He glanced at me and gave me a quick smile. But I couldn't ignore how that glance slipped downward, just for an instant. I kept walking, keeping my pace steady until we were standing inside the garage. It was just as tidy as I remembered.

"Bah-dee!" Click called to the dog still rolling on the grass. At the sound of his name, he stood up, shook himself out, and ran over to us, dodging the raindrops that were now audibly falling on the driveway. C-Roy chuckled.

"Looks like you've got yourself a green dog."

"Cool," Viktor said. "He'll fit right in with our crew. There's something weird about all of us."

"Yeah? What's weird about you?"

Viktor seemed taken aback for a moment. But he recovered quickly. "Oh, you know. Superpowers. Missing body parts. The usual."

"The usual, eh?" Hanging the coiled cord back on its hook, C-Roy shook his head. He pressed the switch on the wall, causing the garage door to come rumbling down. Then he turned back to us. He hadn't changed much. Then again, he was around twenty-five, so that wasn't surprising. Not as tall as Viktor, but still taller than me, he gave the appearance of a displaced Viking with his blond hair, bright blue eyes, and full beard. He was a little tidier than a stereotypical Viking, though. Unlike many of the guys in the Rift Zone, his hair was cut properly. His beard was trimmed, too. If I were being honest, I would've said he was probably the handsomest guy in Kenyonville. But I certainly wasn't going to say anything like that in front of Viktor.

For multiple reasons.

I dug my hand into my pocket and fished out the note. "We need your help."

"Well, I figured. Why else would you be here?" He held out his hand, so I placed the note into it. As my fingers brushed his, his mouth twitched in a little smile. I quickly drew back as if I'd been burned. He cleared his throat and unfolded the piece of paper.

"Dr. Bryan needs a few things," I said. My voice came out sounding a little tense. I hoped Viktor couldn't tell.

"I see that." C-Roy's brilliant eyes scanned the note. His eyebrows rose. Then he looked at Viktor. "So, what happened to you?"

Viktor didn't answer. He probably didn't realize C-Roy was addressing him.

"Does it matter?" I asked. C-Roy frowned and turned to me.

"I like to know what I'm getting into when I go taking a big risk like this."

"How is it a risk?"

He folded the note and stuck it in his jacket pocket. "Seriously, Léa? You're smarter than that. You shouldn't have to ask." Flipping up his hood, he pulled open the garage's side door and gestured toward the house. "Let's talk inside."

I didn't really want to go into his house, but he was already striding away. Click and Buddy didn't need to be told twice; they both trotted after him. If I didn't want to have to explain a lot of stuff to Viktor at that very moment, I was going to have to follow. So I pulled up my hood and took a deep breath.

"Let's be quick. I don't want your gauze getting too wet."

He nodded, but he didn't move.

"Viktor, let's go."

"Are you all right?"

"Yeah. I'm fine. But we can't stand in C-Roy's garage all day."

He frowned. "Is he devastatingly handsome or

something? Because if you want to dump me for him, you can."

"You and I would have to be together for me to dump you."

"So we're *not* together?"

"Viktor." I pulled away a little so I could face him straight on. "We're just friends. Okay?"

"You and I are just friends? Or you and C-Roy?"

"You and I."

"So are you and C-Roy . . ."

I didn't say anything. His mouth dropped open a little.

"Léa," he whispered.

"That was a long time ago."

"What happened?" His expression darkened. "What the fart happened? Did he hurt you? He must've hurt you, or you wouldn't—"

"He didn't hurt me." I sighed and looked toward the side door of the house, which was still open, waiting for us. "I probably hurt him. I don't know. It doesn't matter now."

"Are you going to get back together?"

I shook my head, forgetting he couldn't see that. "I don't know, Viktor."

He just stood there, stunned. I knew he didn't understand. He *couldn't* understand; I hadn't given him enough information. And I still had to keep some of those cards close to my chest if I wanted him to cooperate.

"It's complicated," I said at last.

"You should've told me."

"And you should've told me a lot of things. We're all guilty of keeping secrets."

"I was trying to protect you."

"Maybe I was trying to protect you, too."

"From what?"

I bit my lip and looked away so I wouldn't have to see his face. "You liked me. If you'd known about C-Roy . . . wouldn't that have hurt?"

"Why? Because you had a normal-looking boyfriend?" He pressed his lips together for a moment, as if to quell the shaking. "I bet he has smooth skin. And facial hair. And two eyes."

"Most guys do," I said, the words out before I could stop them. He flinched. "Jesus, Viktor. None of this is about appearances. If it were, I never would've left C-Roy in the first place."

"So he's handsome."

"Yeah, he is. So what? He's not perfect. There are things about him I could do without. Believe me." I looked up at him as he stood there. He looked like he was trying not to cry. "You're not ugly, okay?"

He turned his head away. His hands were clenched in tight fists. It didn't look like he was breathing.

"I'm not just saying that to make you feel better. You're . . . kind of hot."

"Spit." The word came out almost literally. "Don't farting lie to me, Léa."

"I'm not. There's plenty to like. You're tall, dark, and—"

"—mangled." He turned back to face me. A single tear rolled down his cheek from his cloudy eye, trying to find a path through the lumpy channels of scar tissue. "Blind. Stupid."

"You're not stupid."

He swiped his hand over his cheek, brushing the tear away. "I'm sorry. For everything. I'm sorry for causing the Rift. I'm sorry for bringing you back into the Zone. I'm sorry for burdening you with my sorry butt."

"You must be *really* sorry if your butt can feel it."

He shook his head, ignoring my attempt at a joke. "I ruined your life."

I took his hand and placed it on my elbow. "You didn't ruin it," I said. "You just changed it."

"In the worst way," he said miserably. But he didn't resist as I led him out of the garage, closing the door behind us.

CHAPTER 15

BACK IN TIME

It was strange the way the smells of houses stuck in your memories. As soon as I stepped inside C-Roy's place, a lot of stuff came flooding back. My toe—or, at least, the spot where it had been—started to throb.

"Shoes off," C-Roy said as he shucked his own slip-on sneakers. He shoved them onto the doormat with one foot while simultaneously pulling off his jacket and hanging it on a hook just inside the door. I gave him a dirty look. "I'm trying to keep the floors clean."

"Yeah. Sure you are."

He folded his arms across his chest. It looked like he'd kept up with his workouts. He wasn't exactly burly, but he wasn't a veritable stick insect like Viktor. He just looked strong . . . and I knew he was. In more ways than one. But he had to be. Bosses couldn't be pushovers.

"We're not going to be here for very long," I said. "Let's just . . . get this over with."

He snorted in amusement. "What do you think's going to happen here, Léa?"

"God knows." I jerked my chin over at his jacket, where I knew the note still was. "Can you help Dr. Bryan or not?"

He didn't say anything as he retrieved the piece of paper from the pocket. As he unfolded it and read it again, he nodded.

"Well?"

"Antibiotics and painkillers. Pretty standard stuff. I'll see what I can do."

"Viktor needs them."

"Why?"

"Because the doc just cut out my eye," Viktor said, drawing C-Roy's attention his way.

"Excuse me?"

"Did you think the gauze was a fashion statement?"

"Jesus Christ." C-Roy turned back to the note. Dr. Bryan's appeal was probably making a lot more sense to him now.

"Are you going to help?" I asked. When he looked at me, I raised my eyebrows. "You know Dr. Bryan is right."

"Yeah, I know. But does he know what he's asking of me?"

"Probably. He's not an idiot. He wouldn't ask unless . . ."

Viktor grunted. "Guys, are we still talking about antibiotics? Because it doesn't seem like we're talking about antibiotics."

C-Roy and I locked gazes. It made me shudder, but I held the eye contact for as long as I could. He knew how important this was. He knew Dr. Bryan was right, that Viktor couldn't stay here. But *I* knew C-Roy well enough to know that it wasn't going to be that simple.

Buddy, who had been sniffing around the kitchen, seemed to decide that the pristine space wasn't exciting enough. He went trotting off into the next room, his nose going like a tiny bellows. Click started after him, but I grabbed his arm.

"Stay here." I transferred Viktor's hand to his arm.

"Léa?" Viktor said.

"It's fine. I'm just going outside for a sec." Giving C-Roy a pointed look, I stepped back to the door. He rolled his eyes, but he slipped his shoes on. Then we ducked back out into the rain.

"What's the big secret?" he asked as we stumbled inside the garage. His t-shirt was patterned with raindrops. "Why couldn't we talk in the house?"

"Because Viktor doesn't know yet. And keep your voice down. He's blind. His ears are probably getting super sensitive."

"Jesus, Léa. How is this supposed to work? He's going to know something's up when he goes off with one of my runners."

"So I guess I'm not going with him."

He raised his eyebrows. I could see that much, even in the gloomy light. "Did you think you would be?"

"Not really. But I was *hoping* you would have a heart."

"It has nothing to do with having a heart. Getting one person out is a big enough risk. He needs to go. I get that. But you don't."

"He needs me. If you haven't noticed, he can't see."

"You think a runner can't guide him?"

"I thought more than one person was too big of a risk."

He shook his head. "The runner's just getting him out. He'll be on his own after that."

I gaped. "Are you serious? How's he supposed to manage?"

"Blind people manage all the time."

"Yeah, not blind people who've been blind for a couple of days."

He folded his arms again and stared down at me. "I don't *have* to let anyone out. In fact, I shouldn't even be doing this. If too many people find out about the escape route—"

"I haven't told anyone."

"That's not the point. It's a lifeline. We wouldn't survive with just the crap we get from the checkpoints. Lentils and powdered cheese don't keep people going." His gaze swept over me. "You're a perfect example."

"Excuse me for starving."

He shook his head. "I'm just saying. There are things that make life possible. And things that make life worth living. The checkpoints aren't handing out much of either these days."

"Things like what?"

"Food that actually tastes good. Painkillers. Antibiotics."

My eyes went wide. "They don't give out antibiotics?"

"If they did, don't you think Dr. Bryan would be able to get them for himself?"

I frowned, digesting this new piece of information.

"Sometimes I wonder if they're just waiting until we all die off. Or pick each other off." He glanced back toward the house. "Why did Dr. Bryan have to remove Viktor's eye?"

I chewed on my lip. I couldn't very well tell him the truth, because that would bring up the question of why it had happened. And if C-Roy knew he was helping in the escape of the person who'd been the reason why Kenyonville needed an escape route in the first place . . . I wasn't sure what he would do, actually. But I didn't want to risk finding out.

"An accident," I said at last.

"An accident."

"We were foraging. A branch got him in the eye."

He shook his head. "Jesus, Léa. Foraging? If you were that desperate—"

"Well, I'm desperate now. So, are you going to help him?"

"Yeah. I'll help him." He looked down at me. "And you . . ."

"What do you want?" I asked, even though I already knew. He reached out and tucked my hair behind one ear. The gesture was gently familiar, but all I could think about was how similar it was to what Charity had done right before she'd burned her thumbprint into my cheek. C-Roy frowned and leaned a little closer to peer at my face.

"You really *were* desperate," he said softly, his thumb brushing over the new skin. I reached up and grabbed his wrist so I could pull his hand away. He smiled. "Don't worry. I won't ask anything like that of you."

"Oh, I know. That's not your thing."

The smile died from his eyes, though it remained on his lips. "My thing could be worse," he said.

—

had to take my shoes off. There was no way around it. For maybe the first time, I regretted not accepting those socks that Viktor had offered to me months earlier. At least my missing toe would've been somewhat hidden.

I tried not to think about it as I helped Viktor get his boots off. C-Roy led us into the living room . . . which actually still looked like a living room. I knew this was his parents' house; they'd left him in charge of it, much like Niesha's parents had done with theirs. And he'd done a surprisingly good job of keeping everything intact. Given the parties that he liked to throw from time to time, it was amazing there wasn't more damage. Aside from one small dent in the wall—that I knew had been caused by furniture rearranging rather than roughhousing—the place looked pretty good. I helped Viktor over to the navy couch where we both sat down. Click plunked himself on Viktor's other side . . . and Buddy promptly jumped up after him.

"Get down," I said, waving at him with my hand. C-Roy just glanced at the dog and shook his head.

"It's fine. As long as he doesn't pee on the cushions."

"He never has," I said, somewhat offended on Buddy's behalf.

"Has he been on a lot of couches lately?" Turning back to the mantel, he grabbed a remote that was sitting there. The huge TV above the fireplace lit up with a blue screen and a DVD logo.

I frowned. "What are you doing?"

"You guys look awful. Relax and watch a movie."

"Um . . ." Viktor said. I shot C-Roy an annoyed glare.

"That's what descriptive video is for," he said. "Better get used to it." He opened up a cupboard in the built-in shelving, revealing an impressive collection of movies. "Any preferences?"

"Got anything dystopian?" Viktor asked. C-Roy turned to him with a quirked eyebrow.

"Kenyonville isn't dystopian enough for you?"

"Technically, it's post-apocalyptic."

"If you want to get nit-picky." He turned back to the selection and pulled out a box. "This should work." He slipped the disc into the player, then handed the remote to me as he walked past. "I'll get the snacks."

Buddy's ears perked up. He stayed where he was, standing on the cushion beside Click, but he followed C-Roy with a hungry gaze until the guy disappeared around a corner.

"Do you really want to watch this?" I asked Viktor quietly, setting the remote on the arm of the couch.

"I *can't* watch it."

"You know what I mean."

He shook his head. "I'd rather have a nap."

"So have a nap."

"I don't think I'd be able to." He reached up and rubbed his fingers on his forehead above the gauze.

"Is the pain bad? I could ask C-Roy for something. He probably doesn't have anything strong enough, but even an aspirin might—"

"It's okay." He groped toward me with one hand. Sensing what he wanted, I grabbed it and held it tightly. "I guess we're not going back to the doc's tonight, eh?"

I shook my head. "I was hoping C-Roy would have what he needed here. But . . . it looks like we'll have to wait."

"Is he going to let us crash here for the night?"

"If he wasn't, we wouldn't be sitting here right now. He's nothing if not a decent host."

"Decent?" C-Roy called from the kitchen, causing me to jump. "Nice, Léa."

Viktor snorted. "Busted."

I disentangled my fingers from his and stood up. He leaned forward as if he were about to follow, but I pushed him back onto the cushions. "Stay there. I'll help him with the snacks."

"Cheeznudles?"

"You wish." I stepped past his legs, giving Click a pointed look as I went. He gave me a thumbs up, so I hurried to the kitchen.

C-Roy was just pulling some mugs from one of the upper cupboards. There was already a bowl sitting on a tray on the island, and it was full of corn chips. A smaller bowl of salsa sat beside it. My jaw dropped.

"What?" he asked when he saw my expression.

"Things have really improved since I was last here."

"We got the supply chain worked out." He turned to the fridge and pulled open the door. The inside wasn't packed . . . but it was still a lot fuller than I would've expected. He pulled out a bottle of pop and handed it to me.

"So you use the supply chain to import decent junk food?"

"Among other things."

I shook my head as I cracked open the cap. A satis-fying hiss emanated from the bottle. "Don't let Joshua know what you've got or his runners will be on you like flies on shit."

"Oh, he knows. And he also knows to keep his nose out of my business if he doesn't want it to get singed." He slid the mugs toward me so I could pour the fizzing liquid into them, just as there was an unintelligible squawk from behind him. Turning, he grabbed the walkie-talkie from the counter and pressed a button on the side. "Copy that."

"You understood what he said?"

He smirked. "You didn't?"

"Whatever." I focused on pouring the drinks. When that was done, I capped the bottle and returned it to the fridge. C-Roy watched me, his gaze hot against my skin. As I turned back to the island, he gently grabbed my wrist. "I knew you'd come back."

"Oh, so you're psychic now?"

"No. But I know that most of the Rift Zone is a shit-hole. And you don't do shitholes."

"Then what am I doing back here?"

He smiled and let go of my wrist. "There are worse territories. With worse bosses."

"There are better bosses, too."

"Yeah. How *is* Niesha, by the way?"

I blinked. "What do you mean?"

"Last I heard, she skipped town. I'm not sure *how* she did it. As far as I know, we've got the only escape route."

"Maybe she just walked up to a checkpoint and asked nicely."

"So the story goes. But I don't buy that. Do you?"

I looked at the corn chips. My nose seemed to be more sensitive than normal. Either that or I was really hungry, because they were all I could smell. "You wouldn't believe me if I told you."

"Try me."

I shook my head before turning to look at him. He held the walkie-talkie casually, pressing the thick antenna against the underside of his chin. "Maybe I walked up to a checkpoint and asked nicely, too."

"And they didn't let you out for some reason?"

"They let me out. But I came back."

He snorted and pointed the walkie-talkie at me. "Nice try, Léa. But you're not that much of an idiot."

"You have no idea how much of an idiot I am." I picked up the mugs and arranged them on the tray, careful to keep the weight evenly distributed. "I'm here, aren't I?"

He didn't say anything for so long that I was afraid I'd really pissed him off. But when I dared to look up at him, he was just watching me with a puzzled expression.

"Yeah, you're here. You really like this kid, don't you?"

I shook my head. "Is it really any of your business?"

He wiggled the walkie-talkie. "*This* is my business. And if you want my help, I need some answers."

"You don't need to know how I feel about Viktor."

"Don't I?" He shook his head slowly. "You know how this works, Léa. I don't work for free."

"Do we look like we have anything to give you?" I asked, hoping to steer the subject of compensation to something more material than what I knew he really wanted. There was still that watch in Viktor's pocket. But, as I saw C-Roy's expression change, I realized I wasn't going to get away with that. I sighed.

"Good. We understand one another."

"You're a fucking pervert," I whispered, keeping my voice low so that Viktor wouldn't hear. C-Roy just laughed, not bothering to try to hide it.

"Believe me, Léa, there's far worse than me out there." He gestured to the tray. "Go on. Have your snack and watch a movie. I'll make the arrangements. You don't need to worry your pretty little head about anything."

I narrowed my eyes. "You expect me to thank you?"

"Not at this very moment. There'll be time enough for you to show your gratitude later. After."

I swallowed hard. Things had just gotten very, very real.

"If you want to help him," he said, "you know the terms."

"What about Click?"

"He can stay. As long as *you* hold up your end of the bargain." He gave me a little salute with the walkie-talkie as he walked out of the room, heading for the stairs.

"When?" I blurted. He paused, glanced into the living room, then turned back to me.

"Tonight. At nine." Then he was gone, leaving me alone in the kitchen to listen to the bubbles popping in the mugs.

—

Click was fascinated by the pop. He drank all of his mug so fast that there was an inevitable burp a few seconds later that nearly shook the walls. Viktor snorted, then started to laugh.

"Léa? Was that you?"

"Fuck off."

Click's eyes were bright as he eyed my mug. I'd only drunk about half of my pop. It seemed so sweet. Too sweet. So I handed it over to Click. The movie was playing, but the sound was turned down so low that none of us could hear it. I didn't really care about movies. Viktor didn't seem to care about this one, either, even though he'd suggested the genre. In silent agreement, we lay down on the couch, our bodies curled together. He lay behind me with his arms looped around my shoulders. He was still uncomfortably warm—his fever seemed to be going strong—but the day had turned cool, and a lot of the windows in C-Roy's house were open . . . so I didn't mind. And I didn't mind when he pressed his face against the back of my neck, breathing deeply.

Since stepping back into C-Roy's house, a few things had become clear. What I didn't want. What I did. It was almost a relief to admit it to myself after so many months of trying to deny it. Of trying to be brave, and independent, and tough, when all I really wanted was for someone to tell me that everything was all right. That I was going to be all right. That I *was* all right.

Even though I was in C-Roy's house, facing an uncomfortable future, lying in the arms of a broken boy, I felt safer than I had ever felt before in the Zone. For the first time since the Rift, I felt secure. In that moment, I was safe. In that moment, I was happy. In that moment, I knew I was loved by *someone*.

And I was only hours away from losing all of it.

CHAPTER 16

THE AGONY OF GOODBYE

Night crept in slowly in the summer . . . before rushing in all at once with cooler air and the fragrant exhalations of freshly mowed front lawns. I must've fallen asleep; when I opened my eyes, the room was dimly lit in nothing but the blue glow of the TV screen. The movie was probably long over. We'd missed the whole thing.

Viktor was still behind me, his arms wrapped around my shoulders. As I stirred, he let out a warm breath on the back of my neck.

"Feel better?" he asked.

"About what?"

He grunted softly in amusement. "After your nap." His fingers found my shoulder and gave it a squeeze. "You were really snoring there for a while."

I didn't know if he was teasing me. I didn't really care. Carefully, I sat up and looked around the room.

Through the windows, I could see that the streetlights were on. Click was lying on the floor; the only reason I could see him was because he was in a pool of illumination below the window. Buddy lay curled up on the chair behind him, fast asleep.

"Where's C-Roy?" I asked.

"Around here somewhere. I can hear someone moving around upstairs." Viktor sat up slowly, letting out a little groan. "Fart. My head hurts."

"Your head? Or your eye?"

"Can't tell. It's just one big ball of pain."

I wasn't sure whether to be worried about that or not. Never having lost an eye myself, I had no idea if what he was feeling was normal.

"C-Roy said he'd be back at nine. What happens at nine?"

"How should I know?" I said, even as my mouth went dry. I peered at Viktor in the darkness. His gauze pad almost seemed to glow. I stood up and walked over to the lamp on the side table. After a few seconds of fumbling, I managed to turn it on.

"Firing squad?"

"Huh?"

"At nine."

"Why would there be a firing squad?"

"Well, you sound awfully worried about something."

"I'm not," I lied. Even to my own ears, I was anything but convincing. But I was saved from having to make up any excuses by the sound of footsteps thumping down the stairs. I turned and saw C-Roy. He crooked his finger at me.

"Let's go," he said. "Viktor, too."

"Are you *sure* there's no firing squad?" Viktor asked. He was trying to keep his tone light, but I could tell he was nervous. I grabbed his hand and pulled him up off the couch.

"I promise," I said. "No firing squad. Come on." I led him back to the kitchen where C-Roy was just opening the side door. The sound of a gentle rain poured in from outside, accompanied by the tang of petrichor.

"Ready?" a new voice asked. I peered into the darkness and spotted a shadowy figure. C-Roy waved his hand.

"Not quite. Get in here. And stay on the mat."

"Aye, aye." The figure stepped into the kitchen and pushed back the hood of their jacket. I could see that it was a boy, probably around Viktor's age. He was skinny, but not in a starved way. He looked like he'd probably just gone through a growth spurt and had only grown in one direction: up.

C-Roy handed him a folded piece of paper. It wasn't Dr. Bryan's list. "Make sure you check carefully this time," he said. "They shorted us with the last shipment. And make sure they know I added a few new items."

The kid opened the paper and squinted at it, holding it close to his nose. "Amoxicillin?"

"For Dr. Bryan. He needs a few things. They're all on there."

"Wait a sec," Viktor said slowly. We all turned to him. He kneaded my elbow with his fingers. "How long is it going to take to get that stuff?"

"A week," C-Roy said. "If we're lucky."

"So why are we . . ." He trailed off, frowning. "Why didn't we just deliver the list and go? We can come back in a week."

C-Roy stared at him for a moment, then turned to me. "Seriously, Léa?"

I shook my head, but he made a disgusted noise.

"No, *seriously*? You think I'm going to drag him kicking and screaming?"

"What?" Viktor said, his voice rising a little as he started to freak out. "Who?"

"You," C-Roy said before I could jump in and say anything. "You're getting out of here. Lucky you."

Viktor's cloudy eye went wide, pulling at the scarred eyelid. "I . . . Léa? You're coming too, right?"

"No." My voice was a squeak. I swallowed. "I can't."

"Why not?" He shook his head and took a step back, slipping his hand from my elbow. "No. I'm not going anywhere. I don't need—"

"You need a lot of things," C-Roy said. "And you're not going to get them in the Zone."

"But . . ." Viktor looked in my direction, seemingly searching. But when he couldn't see me, he let out a sob. "Léa, please!"

"You have to go," I said. "I'm sorry."

"You'll be alone."

"No, I won't. I'll have Click. And I'll look after him. We'll look after each other."

"I can look after—"

"No, you can't!" My voice rose. "Don't make this harder, Viktor. Goddamn it. Will you just let us help you?"

"How will this help me?" he wailed. "You saw what it was like out there. You saw how Ramona—"

"I saw someone who cares about you," I broke in before he could say any more and let anything slip. C-Roy gave me an incredulous look. "What?" I demanded.

"You got out?"

"I told you I did." I turned back to Viktor, who was standing there, trembling. I stepped closer and reached up, laying my hands on his cheeks. "You're going to go out there and get help. All right? This is happening, Viktor. Whether you like it or not."

"Why?" Tears cascaded from his eye and ran onto my thumb. "We're a team, remember? If I go . . . you have to come."

"I can't."

"Why not?"

I glanced at C-Roy. "Because I made an agreement."

"With who?"

When I didn't answer, he tried to shake his head.

"No. Please. What kind of agreement? Léa, what kind of agreement?" His breathing hitched. "You don't have to do this for me. I'll be fine. Let's just go back to the doc."

"You have to go, Viktor. C-Roy's runner will take you past the wall. And then you're going to find help, all right? You get back to your family. You live your life. Do that for me. Promise me."

"No." His hands found my face and caressed it. "No, I can't—" He broke off, frowning, as his thumbs brushed my cheeks. "You're crying."

It was too much to hold in. The sob burst out of me.

"Léa. Don't cry. Don't cry. You never cry." He leaned his head down until it touched mine. "You never cry," he whispered.

"You have to go."

"But you never cry."

I pulled back a little. He was so close. His feverish skin almost burned my hands, and I could barely see him past the tears. But I knew that, if I didn't do this, I would regret it. Possibly for the rest of my life.

So I closed my eyes and kissed him.

He was only the second guy I had ever kissed. Somehow, though, it felt like we'd both been doing it forever. I sank into the embrace, tasting the slight saltiness that lingered on his lips—corn chips or tears . . . I couldn't tell. His fingers slid into my hair, holding me in place. I didn't mind. I didn't want that moment to end. I wanted to memorize it, to hold on to every last sensation. The sound of our breaths, synchronized. The taste of his lips on my tongue. The warm medley of scar tissue under my right hand. I wanted it all. Forever. But then he pulled away.

"Why?" he whispered. His next words were distorted by tears. "Why would you do that?"

"Because I love you, Viktor. Whoever you are. Whoever you *were*. I love you. And you need to know that when you go out there. Know that, no matter what happens, there's someone who loves you in this world." I sniffed and pulled away, swiping my hands over my cheeks. When I turned to C-Roy, I expected to see a disgusted look, or at least a smirk. But he was frowning.

"Make sure he gets out safe," he said quietly to the runner. Then he grabbed Viktor's boots and handed them to me. I bit my lip, my throat tight with more unshed tears, as I crouched down. C-Roy helped him balance while I slipped on the boots and tied the laces.

"Say goodbye to Click for me," Viktor said. His mouth trembled as if he were about to ugly cry.

"Don't you want to—" I began, but he shook his head. "Okay. It's okay."

He shook his head again. The runner stepped closer, offering his arm.

I couldn't watch them go. I stepped away and gripped the edge of the counter, closing my eyes. But I couldn't close my ears. The sound of the door closing might as well have been the sound of a jail cell slamming shut.

"I'm sorry, Léa," C-Roy said. A warm, heavy hand

settled on my shoulder. I shrugged it off. "I didn't realize you—"

"Never mind. He's gone now." I opened my eyes and turned to face him. "Do I pay you now or later?"

He blinked. "You want to—"

"No, I don't *want* to. But I made a deal. So are we doing this or not?"

—

We left Click to sleep on the living room floor and went upstairs. C-Roy's bedroom—formerly his parents' room—looked just like I remembered. The walls were bare except for nail holes that spoke of the photographs that had once hung there. Considering what he did in that room, I didn't really blame him for taking them down; photos were almost like an audience sometimes.

He grabbed a pillow from the head of the bed and sat down on the other end with it in his lap. I hesitated, staring at the open door.

"Close it if you want," he said. I shook my head and turned back to him.

"Click's a deep sleeper."

"What about the dog?"

I gave him a funny look. "You care if the *dog* sees what you're doing?"

He didn't answer. Instead, he patted the pillow with one hand. I bit my lip and went to lie down on the bed, positioning my right foot on the pillow. He got a little more comfortable, then slipped his hand behind the pillow to unbutton his shorts. I laid my head back and focused on the chandelier above the bed.

But I couldn't hold back the tears. For more than two years, I hadn't let myself cry at all. I'd built up that levee, hardening it, reinforcing it. And that had worked . . . until Viktor had broken through with a small hole. Now, everything around that hole was crumbling, and fast. It felt like, if I didn't get a handle on my emotions soon, the few tears would turn into a deluge, and I'd never be able to stop it. Pressing my palms over my eyes, I took some deep breaths.

"Jesus, Léa. It's just a foot massage. Do you know how many women would actually be enjoying this right now?"

It's not *just a foot massage, though.* I shuddered and kept my hands where they were. I didn't want to see what he was doing, even though I could feel the movement of one of his hands under the pillow, even as the other one gently rubbed my foot . . . paying particular attention to the scar tissue that was all that remained of my baby toe. It didn't hurt. In fact, there were some numb spots in that area. What I felt was worse than pain. It was the sort of thing that made me want to take a shower . . . even knowing that a shower wasn't going to help.

I moved my hands to my ears and kept my eyes tightly closed. I couldn't hear anything except my own breathing, shaky with tears. His warm hand caressed my foot, his thumb playing over the scar. His movements were getting faster. A little more frantic. It was almost over.

I heard him grunt, even past my hands. He didn't move for a few seconds. I waited, holding my breath. It wasn't until I felt him slide the pillow out from under my foot that I dared to lower my hands. The mattress jiggled as he crawled up the bed and sort of collapsed beside me, breathing hard. I rolled onto my side, away from him.

"It was worth it, though," he said, his voice breathy. "Wasn't it?"

I pressed my hands over my mouth to try to stop the explosion of sobs. I couldn't answer. But it turned out that I didn't need to. Within a few seconds, I heard him begin to snore.

CHAPTER 17

EVERYTHING WE'VE LOST

I didn't sleep. But I didn't move, either. If I went downstairs and accidentally woke up Click, I would have to tell him about Viktor. I wasn't ready to do that yet. I wasn't sure if I ever would be.

The curtains were closed, so I couldn't see outside. All I knew was that it was still dark out there. And still raining. The drops pattered on the roof above us, softly at first, and then a little more forcefully. I thought about Viktor, out there in that, without a hood or an umbrella. His gauze was going to get soaked.

Unless there was a tunnel. I wasn't sure what kind of escape route C-Roy had, but unless it involved ladders or pole vaults, it most likely involved going under the wall. I had visions of a bunch of grubby kids tunnelling their way out of the Rift Zone with rusty spoons, like in a prison-break movie. What was far more likely, though, was that someone had stumbled across an existing tunnel. Or a culvert. Or a sewer pipe.

As long as Viktor got out and got the help he needed, it didn't really matter.

I closed my eyes and tried to imagine what was happening. He would be soaked, most likely. So whoever found him would get him out of the rain. Put him in their car and crank up the heater. Take him to a hospital where the nurses would get him out of his wet clothes, change his bandage, get some antibiotics into him, and call his parents. There would be a tearful reunion. Then the family would make plans for the future: Fit him with an artificial eye. Fix his remaining one. Attempt some plastic surgery for his burn. I didn't know exactly what the doctors would be able to do . . . but even the minimum out there would be more than he could ever hope for in the Rift Zone.

I realized I was smiling as I imagined all this. One moment, I wanted to cry. The next, I was just lying there in C-Roy's bed with this weird smile on my face, inexplicably happy. Maybe the Zone was just so shitty that we had to take happiness where we could . . . even if it didn't belong to us personally.

A squawk from the nightstand made me jump. My heart leapt into my throat, and I sat up, looking around. Spotting C-Roy's walkie-talkie, I let out a subdued groan. I waited a moment, wondering if it was going to make another sound. When it didn't, I slowly lowered myself back onto my side. C-Roy slept on, oblivious (or just passed out after his kinky foot-rub session). I closed my eyes against the light from the chandelier, wondering if I should get up and turn it off, when I heard the telltale sound of dog nails on hardwood. I peered into the shadows of the hallway and spotted Buddy.

"Come here," I whispered, holding my hand out to him. He trotted over, probably thinking I had some food. When he realized my hand was empty, he let out a huff and went on an exploratory loop of the bedroom. I closed my eyes again, just as another squawk emanated from the nightstand. With a groan, I sat up and grabbed C-Roy's shoulder.

"What?" he mumbled.

"Somebody's trying to talk to you."

"Jesus. What time is it?"

"How should I know?"

He rolled onto his back and peered over at the walkie-talkie, just as it let out another squawk. "Damn it." He grabbed it and pressed the button. "What?"

"We've got a problem." The words were clear. Too clear. C-Roy sat up, scratching his fingers through his beard.

"What is it? Unless one of my caches is on fire . . ."

I didn't catch anything that was said next. But C-Roy was obviously adept at translating garbled walkie-talkie speech. He glanced at me, then got out of bed. A moment later, there was a thud as he tripped and stumbled.

"Jesus Christ. What's the dog doing in here?" He hurried to the door.

"What's going on?"

"Stay here, Léa."

My eyes widened. "What's going on?" I asked again. But he didn't answer. I watched him disappear into the shadows. His feet thumped down the stairs. My heart thumped in my chest. I stood up. But then I couldn't seem to move.

Something was wrong. The only thing I could think of was that maybe Viktor had balked at the last minute and refused to leave the Rift Zone. The thought filled me with a mixture of anger and relief, enough that I was able to unstick my feet from the floor and step forward.

I was halfway down the stairs when I heard the kitchen door open and close. I wanted to run down those steps, but I managed to restrain myself somehow. When I reached the bottom, I sidled against the doorway to the kitchen, putting myself in the perfect position to listen.

"What the fuck happened?" C-Roy said, keeping his voice low. I pressed my hand against the wall, hoping to hear Viktor's voice. But all I heard was the kid from earlier.

"Hey, I got the shipment and I delivered the list. What more do you want?"

"I want you to do what I asked you to do."

"I *did*. It's not my fault the fucker went and—"

"Keep your voice down," C-Roy whispered. "Léa will hear you."

"What difference does it make? It wasn't like she was ever going to see him again, anyway."

A spike of panic lodged in my throat. I couldn't breathe. It felt like I'd swallowed a piece of barbed wire.

"What happened?" C-Roy asked again, this time more slowly. As if he didn't really want to hear the answer.

"I got him out. And then . . ."

"And then what?"

"I don't know, man. He just walked out in front of a truck. I wasn't about to stop—"

The world went black for a moment. When I could see again, I found myself halfway to the floor, my knees having gone weak. I let myself go, falling the rest of the way, and collapsed on my hands and knees in the kitchen doorway. C-Roy whirled around, his eyes wide.

"Shit. Léa. I told you to—"

"You left him there?" My voice was weirdly high, like I'd inhaled helium. I fixed my gaze on the kid standing in the kitchen, his dark jacket still sparkling with rain. "You left him there?"

"What else was I supposed to do?"

"You don't let him jump in front of a fucking truck!" My hands flared so suddenly that it hurt. It hurt so much that I felt myself pull out of my body, and I watched from the outside as I stood up, staggered a few fury-sharpened steps, and hurled two Riftballs right at the kid.

"Holy shit, Léa!" C-Roy shouted as the kid crashed into a cupboard in his desperate attempt to throw himself out of the way. Neither ball of pink hit its mark. But I wasn't done yet. I advanced, my hands already reloaded. The kid ducked behind the island.

I wanted to scream at him. I wanted to call him the worst names I could think of. But I was no longer in control. There was just rage and anguish and guilt. And a gaping absence that I knew would only grow more unbearable as time went on. My body, still under the control of that mysterious force, rounded the corner of the island. I didn't even have time to register the figure on the other side before the Riftball spun out toward me. It felt like a spike-studded bowling ball as it crashed into my jaw, knocking me off my feet. I fell to the hard kitchen floor, my consciousness slamming back into my body the instant I hit the ground.

"Shit, shit, shit," C-Roy panted, crawling over to me. "What the fuck is wrong with you?" he shouted. I had no idea who he was talking to. I could barely hear him. My face felt like it was melting. The flesh was melting off the bones. It had to be. The burning didn't stop. It was going to devour me.

The scream that came out of my body rattled the windows. C-Roy tried to gather me into his arms, but I threw up my still-flaring hands, smacking him in the chest. He shouted in pain and scrambled back. I let my hands crash to the floor. I didn't feel it. All I could feel was the pain in my face and the pain in my heart, one boring into me from the outside, the other dissolving me from within.

"Lee-ah?"

I couldn't stop screaming. I didn't even know where I was anymore. Everything was too dark. Too bright. Too cold. Too hot. Too painful. A single thought entered my head, swam around for a moment, and then settled.

I want to go, too.

It was strangely calming. The thought that this burn might be enough to make my wish come true gave me a fleeting moment of peace. I sucked in a breath and let out another scream. But it sounded tired. Resigned. Tears leaked from my closed eyes as I lay there on C-Roy's kitchen floor, utterly alone. Utterly bereft. Sobs shook me so hard that my ribs banged against the floor. Everything hurt. Why did everything have to hurt so much? Strangely, though, I started to feel something soft. Something familiar. Opening my eyes, I blinked away the tears to find Click kneeling beside me. Both of his hands hovered just over my cheek, and as I heard the soft hum, I understood what he was doing.

"No. Don't."

His eyes remained closed. He didn't listen. His hands stayed right where they were, pouring that balm-like energy right into my skin. I let out a sob.

"Click, stop."

He didn't.

"Viktor's gone."

He opened his eyes. I fixed my gaze on his golden one.

"He's dead," I whispered.

"Vee-kah." He moved one hand to his chest for a moment. "Vee-kah," he repeated, and placed that same hand on my chest. It jerked as I tried to take a deep breath.

"Don't you care?"

He closed his eyes again and resumed his healing work. The burn was tingling. Tickling. Healing. But I didn't want it to heal. I sat up and grabbed his wrist, glaring at him through streaming eyes.

"I said, stop."

"Léa," C-Roy said. I turned to where he was crouched. He looked terrified and bewildered. He'd forgotten to button his fly. That little detail stuck in my head, making a mockery of the situation. Of my pain.

"Fuck you."

"I know." He shook his head. "Let him heal you. Whatever he's doing, it's—"

"Fuck you!" I shouted, letting go of Click's wrist. "I was trying to help Viktor. You were supposed to get him out. Not—"

"I know." He turned and looked at the kid who was cowering behind the island. "Get out."

He gaped. "It wasn't my fault! She's fucking crazy, C-Roy."

"Get out. Now!"

The kid scrambled to his feet, keeping a wary eye on me, and hurried for the door. As soon as it slammed, C-Roy turned back to me.

"I'm sorry, Léa. This wasn't supposed to happen. You have to believe me."

I did believe him. And that was the problem. "None of this was supposed to happen," I whispered. Reaching up, I touched the side of my face. Click's hand shot out to grab my wrist before I could do any more than brush the sticky tissue.

"Lee-ah," he said, his voice soft. "Vee-kah." He placed his hand on my chest again. I nodded, then looked away as the tears cascaded from my eyes. They stung as they dribbled into the burned tissue.

Oh, god, they stung.

"What can I do?" C-Roy asked. "Let me help. You can stay here as long as you want. No strings attached. You can have the guest room. Just . . . let me help you."

"I've had enough of your help." I bowed my head over my lap. Click's gentle fingers tucked my hair back behind my ear; a moment later, I could feel that soft, cuddly fuzz of energy once more. "I just want to go home."

The room was silent. I closed my eyes.

"I'm going home," I whispered.

ALSO BY NISSA HARLOW

Two Between Worlds
The Last Minute
No Such Thing
Elements of Mind: The Complete Quartet

Generation Rift
Nothing Close to Home
Escape From the Zone
So Lost Are the Foes
All the Scars of Hope

ABOUT
THE AUTHOR

Nissa Harlow wanted to be a writer from the time she was a small child, but it took a while before she finally did anything about it. In the meantime, she worked as a volunteer day-camp counsellor, a movie extra, and a digital-photo editor. She even once worked on a conveyor belt in a chocolate factory (which was as stressful—and delicious—as it sounds).

These days, she lives in British Columbia, Canada and writes stories about friendship, love, and healing, all embellished with a touch of the fantastic.